A CARTER PUBLICATION PRESENTS

JOE CARTER

THE
A Jordan Jones Novel
CROSS KILLINGS

ISBN: 1451518811
ISBN-13: 9781451518818

A CARTER PUBLICATION

Edited by Lisa Klinge, Kristina Sowell and Shera Coleman

Authors note

I want to thank everyone who supports A CARTER PUBLICATION, this is the first of many book titles in my arsenal. The suspense will have you turning pages till the end.

Prologue

The body hanging was lifeless, its dark blood dripping from its head, torso, hands, and feet. Before it, a young man knelt in the shadowy room.

"God, forgive me, for I have sinned. I offer this sacrifice to you."

He got up, tugged his clothes over his bloody body, and took one more look at the pale, curvaceous young woman, before he closed the door of her apartment behind him.

Chapter 1

—

THE ABDUCTION

Thursday night the van circled the block three times before it slowed to a stop at the curb. The driver had been stalking the woman for three days just looking for an opportunity to strike; now, he was ready to make his move. The voice was constantly in his ear, chanting, "Her- she's the one, she's the one." He went into the back of the van to grab a piece of cloth and a small bottle of chloroform, waiting anxiously for her to leave the store where she worked. As part of his plan, he had parked the van on the block she took on her way to the train station. The anticipation was making his skin feel like there were a million little needles pricking at it. He picked up his binoculars and watched her walk around the store with a clipboard and pen doing inventory, just as she'd done the past two nights. Then again the voice spoke to him, again and again he kept chanting, "Her- she's the one. She's the one."

She dialed the phone and talked no more than six or seven minutes, like she'd done each night when he'd timed the call. Then, she put on her red coat and wrapped a blue scarf around her neck. When she turned off the store lights, he exited the van, leaving the side door open. He then walked into a dark doorway directly across from the van. He'd broken the light that covered the area last night. He waited. His plan so far was working. He took a peek to see if she was coming – she was locking the door. Making sure it was secure, she pulled down on the lock to see if it would open, it was locked. This was it, the time he was waiting for, his breathing became heavy, his heart pumping. The excitement was rushing through his body, he wanted to just run up to her and snatch her off the street, but the fear of being seen stopped him. It felt like hours had passed by, but it was only minutes. She was getting closer; his heartbeat matched her pace of walking, closer, closer. He pulled the cloth from his pocket, soaked it with the chloroform, and continued to wait. She came up the block with her hands in her coat pockets. Her eyes were focused on the train station; she had two blocks to go. When she walked directly in front of him, he grabbed her from behind and pulled her into the doorway with him. Lifting her a foot and a half off the ground, he put the cloth over her nose and held it tightly. Her eyes opened widely as if she could use them to scream for help. She struggled, the strong fingers pressed up against her mouth and nose applying more pressure, he wanted to bash her head up against the brick wall behind him, to stop her feeble attempts of trying to free herself, but he needed her to be undamaged.

Kicking, trying to scream, she desperately tried to get away, until she couldn't struggle anymore. She fell limp into his arms, and he put her into the van, tied her up and drove off. Only the sound of the van's tires turning through wet streets disturbed the silence.

Chapter 2

—

SCARED TO DEATH

Disoriented, she tried to adjust her eyes to the darkness, but she still couldn't see anything. Her naked body was shivering from the cold air that sounded like it was blowing through open windows. What her neck, hands, and feet were strapped to, she didn't know. The last thing she remembered was being grabbed on her way to the train station.

"Hello, is anyone there? Please don't do this...please... please...help me...please help...help...help."

Her cries for help went unnoticed. The strap holding her neck in place was so tight that it pressed down on her throat, making her cries sound low. Her eyes were bloodshot red and tears poured down her face. She tried to move her head to look around, but her neck and head were strapped too tight. The strap ripped her skin, and blood spotted her face. She couldn't move, except for the uncontrollable shaking of her body. She could feel tiny pins...splinters, she thought, sticking into her body. She tried again to free herself from the straps, but a light flashed into her face so brightly she couldn't open her eyes. When the light went off, she opened them and was staring into the eyes of her kidnapper.

"Do you know that Jesus was crucified for our sins, and we take what happened to him for granted?"

"Please, I'll do anything you want, just let me go. I won't tell anybody, please...God help me." Her eyes frantically moved back and forth as she tried to look around her.

She could feel his hands repeatedly touching her body and she quivered every time. She wanted to cry out, but when she tried, the strap pushed down on her throat, choking off her words. She twisted her hands and legs to see if she could loosen the straps, but it didn't do any good.

He spoke again. "I've tried to deal with the pain, but it's too much to bear. I tried to deal with the agony but I can't anymore...it's time I make the pain go away. It hurts so much...why should I suffer while there are so many sinners out there that deserve to feel what I feel? They're the ones that should pay, not me. You should pay, and others like you."

Then there was silence again as he moved away and just stared at her. She screamed as loud as she could, but her screams were still muffled by the strap. Aggravated, he smacked her across the face so hard that he knocked her out.

When she regained consciousness, she could feel a wet, throbbing ache above her left eye, and her entire face hurt. Her hands were shaking; her body was trembling uncontrollably. She immediately started to shake, trying to free herself again. He unfastened the strap holding her neck, and she screamed as loudly as she could, her mouth wide open, baring her upper and lower teeth, her hair wild, and the whites of her eyes bulging.

With one powerful swing he slit her throat, and there was silence. The blood squirted all over his face. He stood there and relished it for a moment, then continued to mutilate her body. He took his clothes off, revealing his long, muscular frame. He got on his knees, cupped his hands, and let blood fill them. Then, he smeared the blood on his face and on his body.

The more blood he smeared on his body, the more he felt his pain slowly fade away. He was totally covered in blood, and he watched the scars on his body disappear.

"God, forgive me, for I have sinned. I cannot take the pain any longer. I'm not worthy of the gift you have given me. I give this woman as my gift to you. I use her blood to wipe my pain away. But I offer her body and soul to you, so that the pain Jesus Christ endured does not go in vain."

Covered in her blood, he knelt in front of her body for an hour, looking at her. As the blood dried, it became a dark red, crusted shell on his body, and for a moment, he looked confused. He gathered his thoughts and carefully put his clothes on, walked to the door, opened it, and left the apartment.

Unnoticed, he left the building, got into his van, and turned on the wipers, watching them push away the small drifts of snow on the windshield. He put the van in gear, and it pushed its way through the four inches of snow and into the night.

The drive to his place of dwelling was quiet, the streets were empty. He rolled down the windows and heard the sound of his tires turning repeatedly on the wet streets. The lights were synchronized, they all turned green once he made the first right turn. Moving at a high speed an hour later he was at his place of residence. He parked the van, and went inside, his room was empty, the walls barren. The only thing that stood out was a Bible that took its place on the empty floor, nothing surrounding it, and a chair facing the window.

He went into the shower, stood and let the water wash off the dried, crusted blood. Small pieces of blood fell onto the shower floor like chipping plaster pieces falling off a wall. He watched as the water turned red, slowly swirling down the drain. Afterwards, he entered his room naked, picked up the Bible and read into the night.

Chapter 3

—

SNOW DAY

Friday morning the snow had just stopped coming down, and visibility was a little clearer. Snowplows were all over the city, making the streets safe. After dealing with three accidents and directing cars and pedestrians to safer routes to avoid downtown construction, Officers Wright and Johnson decided to take a break. Wright focused on driving, while Johnson looked out the window. His attention was drawn to several men carrying shovels. Probably looking to make money, he thought. Wright parked their patrol car right off the entrance to Fort Green Park. He kept the engine running and the heat on high. Both officers welcomed the heat. Standing outside as traffic controllers in bad weather was something they both didn't want a part of anymore.

The officers took in some menial conversations, talked on their cell phones until a call came over the radio for a missing person and Johnson picked up the mike. "This is car 331. We'll take the ten-fifty-seven."

"Johnson, you do realize we've been busy all morning? Car 332 or 333 could've taken that call. Now, it looks like we'll be going into overtime, and I was looking to get off on time today."

"We have two hours of tour left, and we could do this in two, easy. We'll go over there, take the report, and leave it for the next shift."

"I hope so, because I got plans this afternoon and I don't want to be stuck doing paperwork for hours."

Wright put the cruiser in gear, turned on the flashing lights, and headed out. Eighteen minutes later, Johnson said, "This is the house... pull over here."

Wright parked the patrol car, and as they both got out, Johnson said, "Heads up. Somebody's coming."

An elderly black woman with a head full of gray hair came out of the two-story home. She was dressed in a white terrycloth housecoat, pink pajamas, and white bunny slippers. She headed towards them. Officer Johnson immediately noticed the worry in her face. She looked as if she had not slept.

"Hello, ma'am. Did you call the police?" Officer Wright said, as he made sure his hat was on straight.

In a nervous, concerned tone, she said, "Yes, I did. My name is Jackie Washington, and my daughter Pamela didn't get home from work last night. Please come in." Her breath had the distinct smell of cigarettes.

Pulling her housecoat tightly around her body, she walked back to the house and held the door open. They followed her inside and unzipped their heavy coats. She led them into the kitchen and continued talking. "My daughter always comes here every night to see if I'm okay."

Officer Johnson pulled out his pad and pen and took notes as Officer Wright asked questions.

"What's your daughter's name?"

"Pamela Washington."

"What's her address?"

"765 Morrison Street."

"That's the Bedford Stuyvesant section of Brooklyn?"

"Yes, it is."

"I need to have a description of your daughter."

"She has light brown skin, short black hair, and she's five feet tall."

Ms. Washington paused for a second, so Officer Wright asked, "So, about how much does she weigh? And doe's she has any distinctive marks?"

"Oh...she's a little thing, maybe a hundred and twenty pounds; she has a tattoo of a heart on her left ankle."

"Ms. Washington, do you have a recent picture of your daughter?"

She went into the living room and took a photo off the floor model TV. She brought it back to Officer Wright, who pulled the photo out of the frame and laid it on the kitchen table.

Officer Wright asked, "Now, is there a chance she stayed at a friend's house because of the weather?"

"She would've called me and told me something; she just wouldn't stay out all night and not tell me. I already called the one person she would've called, and she hasn't heard from her since yesterday afternoon. I also called her job, and they told me she closed the store last night, but other than that they wouldn't know where she went or where she could be. I also called her apartment and didn't get an answer. Please, can you two go and check her home? I'm unable to travel by myself and my attendant isn't due here until later on."

Officer Wright said, "We'll take a ride over there. But, I need to ask you a few more questions first, okay? What's her place of employment and the address?"

After getting all the information the officers needed, Officer Wright said, "We'll give this information to the detective squad, but you'll need to go down to the police station to file a missing person report. You'll have to understand that a person has to be missing seventy-two hours at least. That's the legal amount of time until a person can be declared missing, unless there's evidence of a crime. Here are numbers of two detectives who work cases like these. Let them know I referred you to them."

Officer Wright and Johnson never went to Pamela's apartment, and two and a half hours later, Ms. Washington walked into the Eighty-Fourth Precinct.

Visibly frail, Ms. Washington patted her eyes with her handkerchief and waited for someone to help her. A uniformed officer came over to her.

"Hello, ma'am. Are you being helped?"

"No. Can I speak to Detective Jordan Jones or Detective Maxwell Brown?"

"May I ask who is asking?"

"Ms. Jackie Washington. I was referred to them by Officers Wright and Johnson."

"Let me go see if they're available."

The officer left and came back ten minutes later with a very well dressed Detective Brown. An avid football fan, Ms. Washington was surprised by his resemblance to Tiki Barber, running back for the New York Giants.

The officer bent down to talk to Ms. Washington.

"Hello, ma'am. This is detective Maxwell Brown, one of the detectives you were asking about. He'll help you."

As Ms. Washington was getting up, she held out her hand to Brown for support, Ms. Washington's aide sat patiently awaiting her return. Detective Brown helped her to her feet. She said, "Thank you, detective," and he shook her hand, and escorted her upstairs to a chair in front of his desk. "Have a seat, Ms. Washington. So, how can I help you?"

Pushing aside case files and stacks of paper, Brown sat down and leaned forward with his elbows on the desk.

In an unsteady voice, Ms. Washington told Brown the same story she had given Officers Wright and Johnson earlier.

"The time period before we can officially file a missing person's report is seventy-two hours, but let me take some information from you, and I'll see what I can do, ok?" Brown said.

"Ok." Ms. Washington replied.

Brown picked up a pad, took a pen from his shirt pocket and started to ask her questions. After getting all the information he needed, "We'll do what we can, but I believe she's ok…probably got caught up in the moment. Do you have a photo of her?"

She gave him a current photo of Pamela. Brown took a second just to focus on it and laid it down on his desk. He had a knack for remembering faces, something he had picked up on the job. Getting up and buttoning his suit jacket, Brown said, "Ms. Washington, we'll do what we can. You'll have to remember, though, she has to be missing at least seventy-two hours, but I'll look into it, ok?"

"Thank you very much."

"I wouldn't worry too much about this. It's the weekend, Christmas is coming up, and she's probably just lost track of time having fun. I'm going to write up a report. If you don't hear from her by Sunday night, come back and see me Monday morning."

"Maybe you're right – it's just that she has never done this before."

Detective Brown walked with Ms. Washington down the stairs and to the front of the precinct. He held the heavy silver door open for Ms. Washington and watched her as she got into a waiting yellow cab.

Detective Brown was given a slip of paper by his Captain as he walked back to his desk and was told, "I couldn't get hold of your partner, but you and Jones are up something crazy I hear. Grab your partner and get to that address a.s.a.p."

"Yes sir." Brown sat at his desk and pulled out a form and filled in the information provided by Ms. Washington, he took the picture she had given him, clipped it to the form and slipped the items into his desk.

Chapter 4

JORDAN AND TAMERA

The sun shone through the bedroom window, and the smell of cooking food motivated Jones to sit up in bed. Yawning, Jones grabbed the TV remote, flipped it on to the news channel, and yelled out, "Tamera, why did you let me sleep so late?"

Tamera came into the room wearing his New York Giants jersey and nothing else, her body moving like a black cat across the bedroom. She got into the bed and sat next to him. "You looked so peaceful that I didn't want to wake you. I made some breakfast...you hungry baby?"

Jones grabbed her close to him and attempted to get a kiss, but Tamera playfully pushed his lips away. Using her hands, she motioned for him to brush first and started laughing.

"Oh, you got jokes."

Cupping his hands in front of his mouth, he blew into them and quickly pulled his face away. Tamera started laughing again.

"Smells, don't it?"

"I'll be right back." He playfully smacked Tamera on the butt and hurried into the bathroom. When he came back, he jumped back into the bed and asked, "Now, what do you think?" He opened his mouth and used his tongue to wipe his teeth as if he was giving them a shine. Tamera bent over to smell his breath.

"Much better, detective."

Jones lifted her up and pulled her onto his lap…the anticipation of making love to her was overwhelming. He was ready, and from the look on Tamera's face, he knew she was ready for that early morning thing, too. They kissed each other passionately, both of them enjoying each other's lips. Jones slowly took off the jersey and looked at her breasts with hungry eyes. They were soft and full, and her nipples were hard and sensitive to the touch. He caressed both of them and carefully started to suck on her nipples, one at time. Tamera held her head back and welcomed the satisfaction her body was receiving as her hands caressed his broad shoulders. She could feel him getting harder and harder, rising with every passionate kiss. Jones gently pulled her face in front of his.

"I love you baby, Tamera, and always will. Remember that."

"And I love you, Jordan, with all my heart. I thank God for blessing us both with our love and life."

Their emotions ran high, and at that moment, Jones knew Tamera was the one. Without a doubt, he knew he would always love her. Holding each other's bodies, they were a portrait of perfection. The time was now…right now. He lay on his back and Tamera slowly got on top of him. With her hands, she guided him into her. She moaned in satisfaction. She could feel his strength as she slowly moved up and down in ecstasy, and let out a sigh of relief. Holding her firmly by the waist, Jones pushed up, fully inside her; Tamera pushed down, her hands gripping his strong chest, and then bent down to kiss him.

Locking lips and tongues together, Jones turned her around on her back and pushed even deeper into her. Tamera moved backwards, her head hitting the headboard. She welcomed the powerful thrusts and let out a light scream, tears rolling down her eyes. Her body started to shiver and she felt herself opening even wider. Jones kept pushing and pushing and pushing. Tamera could feel his liquid explode into her body. They froze in their positions mentally and physically, taking in the pleasure.

Moments later, Jones was lying on his back with Tamera's arm across his chest.

"I love you, Jordan."

"I love you, too, baby."

"My head hurts baby."

They both started laughing.

"That's because I know what I'm doing." Tamera playfully hit Jones on his chest and they started laughing again.

They both wanted to stay in bed, but life has to take its course. Jones looked at the clock on the night table; time to get ready. He moved in a little closer and kissed Tamera on the lips. As she lay beside him, he didn't want to leave her side. But he knew he couldn't let her beauty distract him from going to work. He had an important meeting today and wanted to make sure he was on time. Beating on his chest like King Kong, with a growl, "Now I'm hungry, baby."

Tamera was laughing as Jones banged on his chest. She put the jersey back on, grabbed his chin, gave him a kiss, and went back into the kitchen to finish preparing breakfast. After getting up and putting on his robe and slippers, Jones went into the kitchen, and they sat down to eat.

The table was set like they were at a restaurant: everything thought out and carefully placed. Tamera had made pancakes, eggs, beef sausages, biscuits, and a hot cup of hot chocolate, just the way Jones liked it. The smell of the food opened his nostrils, and he fanned it toward his nose. This reminded him of his grandmother's cooking. Even until this day, he knew she could make your eyes eat more than your stomach could hold. He had never thought he would find a woman that cooked like her. They said their prayers and dug in.

"This is good, baby."

"I'm glad you like it."

"So, what do you have planned today?" Jones asked as he cut into his pancakes and stuffed them into his mouth.

"Nothing much, same ol' same ol', this being my last day on vacation I'm going to stop by my mother's house first and run some errands with her. Then, I'm going to see my publisher to discuss some promotional ideas to get my new book off the ground."

"She gets right on the job, huh?"

"Yes, she does. She likes to get an early start; you know, think of ideas and jot them down. And she'll see what will work and what won't, so that everything is thought of in advance."

"Sounds like a good start."

"Yeah, I think so." Cutting into her pancakes, and using her fork she lifted the small pieces of syrup soaked cakes and put them into her mouth and started talking at the same time, grabbing her napkin, preventing the tasty food from escaping her mouth. She grabbed her drink, washed it down and said,

"So it's been three weeks since your big day, Detective."

"Yes it has."

"So what's its like…being a Detective now?" Tamera held her hands under her chin, her pretty eyes fixated on

Jones. Jones picked up his cup of hot chocolate, took a sip, and sat it back down. "It's been quiet so far. We haven't gotten a real homicide case yet."

"So, what are you going to do today?"

"Me...well, the Captain will probably tell the squad a back-in-the-day war story. Then we'll sit around until we get a call or until the Captain gives us a hit. Oh, I meant to tell you one of the secretaries stopped me the other day and said she liked *A King's Palace*."

Jones was now putting grape jelly on his biscuits.

"Oh, she did? Did she say anything about *All Business*?"

"Yes, she did. She bought it and is going to read it. And, I mentioned you're working on your third one."

"That's what I'm talking about, baby...networking for me. I got to put you on my payroll," Tamera said, laughing.

"Hey, it is what it is; my baby is going to be a number-one, bestselling author."

Jones started smiling and moving his shoulders back and forth and snapping his fingers like he was dancing. They both started laughing again.

"So, did you tell Maxwell you moved in with me?"

"Umm...no, not yet."

"Why...is it a man thing?"

"No, it's not a man thing. It just hasn't come up in conversation, and I don't tell him everything, you know."

"I know, I'm just playing. Bet he'll get a kick out of it, though."

"Yeah, knowing Brown, he will – he'll think I'm crazy."

"Just look at it like this: you gave up your player days for me."

"Yes, I did, and I'm glad I did, because you're the best." Jones leaned over the table and gave Tamera a kiss.

"You finished, baby?"

"Yeah, I'm done. That was a good breakfast."

"Thank you."

Tamera got up and started cleaning off the table. Jones picked up the newspaper and started reading, sipping on his hot chocolate. When he was done, he got up and stood behind Tamera as she was drying the dishes. They started play fighting and laughing, with her holding a dishtowel and a plate. He pulled her close to him, turned her around, put two fingers on Tamera's lips, and kissed her. She kissed him back. Then she turned back around and continued drying the dishes. He smacked her on the butt as he left the kitchen.

Jones went into the bathroom, used the toilet, turned on the shower, and got in. The water was warm and the steam made him feel like he was in a sauna. He held his head up so that the water could run down his face. The steam filled the bathroom. He stayed in the shower for at least twenty-five minutes, just absorbing the warm water as it flowed powerfully down his back. Then, there was a knock on the door.

"Jordan…baby, you ok in there?"

"Yeah, I'm ok, pass me a towel."

Tamera went to get a towel, and when she came back Jones was wiping the steam off the mirror with his right hand. Tamera rolled up the towel and snapped it at his butt. Jones turned around and smiled. "Oh, I'm going to get you"

Tamera smiled and tossed him the towel. Jones dried off and wrapped the towel around his body revealing his chest. He stood in front of the mirror and started brushing his hair. He took his electric razor, shaved off the little strands of hair, and moved his face up and down to see if he'd gotten them all – he had. He walked out of the bathroom and Tamera already had his clothes laid out on the bed for him: black blazer, white shirt, black jeans, and all black GBX boots. Tamera sat on the bed and watched Jones as he got dressed. She marveled at his dark brown skin and broad shoulders, washboard stomach, and bulging biceps. Ok…maybe she was exaggerating a little, but he wasn't badly built. When Jones first met Tamera dressed in his uniform, she had asked him if he'd ever seen the movie *Taxi* with Queen Latifah. He told her no and asked her why. She said Jones had a very strong resemblance to Henry Simmons, the man who played Queen Latifah's boyfriend.

Dressed and ready, Jones grabbed his nine millimeter from the nightstand drawer. He usually kept his weapons in a safe in the living room area, but he hadn't really thought about it last night. He put the gun in his holster, clipped it on his belt, and slid it around to his side for easier access. He picked up his snub nose thirty-eight and ankle holster, put the gun in the holster, and strapped it to his right ankle, just above the bone. He grabbed his badge and thought to himself, finally, a homicide detective. He put the badge around his neck and headed for the door.

"Ok, baby, I'll see you later."

"Wait, what time are you getting off work today?"

Tamera got up to her knees and went to him. Jones watched her move swiftly across the bed. She pulled off the jersey, revealing her body. Her black skin glowed, her breasts were full, and her nipples were erect. Her hair, long and thick, fell to her waist. He stood in awe of her body and beautiful smile. She grabbed him by the shirt, put her arms around his neck, and said, "Why, Detective Jordan Jones, what's the matter? You nervous?"

"Girl…there you go, trying to get me all started again, but you know I got to get out of here."

Making sure his tie was tied properly, "Yeah, I know, so what time should I expect you home tonight?"

"About four or five. I have some paperwork to finish, but I'll be home as soon as possible so we can finish this..."

"You promise?"

"You bet."

Jones kissed her on the lips and headed for the door. As he started to open the door, his Blackberry rang, so he answered it.

"Hello?"

"What's up, partner? It's me, Brown."

"This is a surprise. I usually give you the wakeup call. What's up? Everything ok?"

"The meeting this morning was cancelled – we have a homicide case, partner. The word is it's some real psycho stuff. The Captain tried calling you, but he kept getting your voicemail."

"I moved in with Tamera and haven't had the time to change my numbers. My cell doesn't get a good signal in here."

"So, you made the move to move in, and you didn't even tell your partner, your best friend?"

"I just did it over the weekend, you know. Anyway...I'll fill you in later with the details. What info do you have on the case?"

"Nothing other than it's psycho stuff. I'm in the dark on the details…but, it's different, and we got the hit."

Tamera came into the living room from the kitchen, "I'm getting into the shower, Jordan. Make sure you lock the door when you leave, ok?"

"Jones, tell her I said hello and to hook me up with one of her fine-ass friends, partner."

"Brown, her friends think you're a playboy, player." Jones pulled the phone from his ear, "Ok, I'm leaving now. See you later. Love you and Brown says hello."

"Tell him I said hello back."

Jones turned his attention back to Brown, and before he could say anything, Brown started laughing. "That's so cute, I love you… smooch, smooch. She has you trained already, partner."

With a slight grin on his face, he said, "Brown, where are you?"

"I'm on my way to pick you up. I'll be there in about twenty minutes."

"Ok, I'll be downstairs waiting on you, and hurry up, because it's cold out there."

Jones hung up the phone, locked the door, and took the elevator downstairs. He stood in the lobby, looked at his watch, and decided to wait outside. He turned up his collar to protect his neck from the cold. The snow was slowly going away, but there were still piles of it at the end of each corner and in spaces where cars usually parked. Cars were everywhere, making a two-way street look like a one-way street.

Brown pulled up twenty-two minutes later in a black Ford Crown Victoria Interceptor equipped with a shotgun holster and what Brown liked the most about the car, cup holders.

"What's up, Jones?"

"Nothing much," Jones said as he went to the passenger side and got in the car "So, what's this case about?"

"Here, I picked you up a cup of coffee…sergeant Morrison called in a murder, and the captain wants us to handle it. I escorted an elderly woman out of the precinct, and as I was walking back to my desk, he stopped me, gave me the location on a piece of paper, and said you're up."

"So, where are we headed?"

Chapter 5

THE BODY

As Jones and Brown slowly pulled up to a charcoal colored apartment building, Brown put on the siren, strobe and LED lights. They both noticed a crowd of curious bystanders across the street, where Officers Wright and Johnson kept them from crossing the yellow strip barrier tapeline. Brown honked the horn to signal their arrival and continued on. There were three parked police cars, two blocking the cross streets to prevent cars driving up and down the block, and the other in front of the building. Brown parked the car and they got out. A small gust of wind and particles of snow hit their faces as they walked over to the police officers standing in front of the building. Brown took one more sip of his coffee, crumpled the cup, and threw it into a pile of snow as one of the officers walked towards them.

"Sergeant Morrison," Jones said as he held out his hand.

"Jones, Brown, how you guys doing? We got the call at seven AM. I've never seen anything like this before. The coroner said she's been dead at least two days, African

American female about twenty-three. You'll have to see for yourself to understand what I'm saying. The body is on the third floor."

Jones said, "That bad, huh?"

"Worse than bad…I've never seen anything like this in my twenty-some years on the force, and I've seen some doozies."

They walked into the apartment, and Jones smelled the dead body immediately. The kitchen was the first room they saw, and it was nicely kept, everything in its place. Members of the crime scene unit were already there, investigating. The detectives went further into the apartment and entered the living room area. Brown said, "I'd seen *Friday the Thirteenth*, *Freddy vs. Jason*, and *The Texas Chainsaw Massacre,* but this..."

A look of shock washed over their faces as they watched members of the crime scene unit working on a naked black woman with her throat slit. She was strapped to what looked very much like a cross and was displayed like Jesus Christ. The women's mouth was open, and they could see the dried tears on her face. Her neck, mouth, hands, and feet were strapped to the beams, holding her in place. There was a cut on her arms and another from the middle of her chest to her bellybutton. The blood had poured out of her body and formed a pool that was now a thick, red, dry spot on the floor under her dangling feet. The cross was mounted on the wall about two feet off the floor. It looked like a crucifix that would be displayed behind a pulpit in a church. The clothes she'd been wearing were about a foot away. They appeared to have been cut off her body. Brown and Jones gave each other a disturbed look. They put on plastic gloves and walked over to the body to investigate.

Jones said, "Do we have a name for the victim and who discovered the body?"

Sergeant Morrison said, "We do, sir; her name is Vanessa Flores, according to a student I.D. we found in the bedroom. Frank Jefferson found her this way. He's the landlord; he came up here after receiving multiple phone calls reporting a foul odor. He saw this and immediately called the police."

"Is he still here?"

"Yes."

"Make sure he doesn't leave until we speak to him."

"Yes, sir."

"Who would do something like this?"

Brown took a look at Jones and said, "Looks like a hate thing, maybe domestic, you know. Maybe her boyfriend wanted to make a statement, and this is the end result."

"Domestic? I don't think so, Brown…this looks like something else, something monstrous. Whoever did this took his or her time to put her up that way."

"Like something you would see in a movie. Whatever happened to just killing somebody, and that's it? Yeah…this is something out of a *Saw* movie."

"A *Saw* movie?"

Brown opened his left hand and used his right hand fingers to count.

"Yeah…*Saw One*, *Two* and *Three*. The killer was putting people in all sorts of contraptions they had to get out of to survive. You never saw the movie, Jones?"

"No, I haven't, but I'll get around to it."

Brown got a little closer and said, "Well… there aren't any pentagrams, so do we rule out a satanic cult?"

"We'll follow up on everything until we can all agree. Sergeant Morrison, make sure your men interview everybody in this building. If any tenants have a problem with that, let us know."

"Yes, sir."

"What's that she's strapped to?"

"It's wood, Detective, carefully carved into a cross."

Brown and Jones turned to see a woman behind them.

"Hello, Detectives. I'm Julie Torres, I lead this crime scene unit."

After shaking hands with both of them, Torres said, "Detectives Jones, Brown." Her Spanish accent was strong and sexy at the same time, Brown pushed his chest out and his tone of voice was a little different than usual. Brown couldn't help but see the beauty in her. Jones didn't blame him for his change in posture, the voice change was a little over the top but Brown was Brown. Her brown hair came to her shoulders and her pretty face shone in a way that aroused him so he knew Brown was feeling something also.

Jones could tell she had a strong personality. When she turned around to discuss the corpse, she spoke as if she was teaching a class and they were her students. Jones rubbed his hand on the wood.

Brown said, "Why is she so stiff?"

"*Rigor mortis.*"

"Excuse me?" Knowing full well what *rigor mortis* meant, Brown just wanted to hear her talk.

"*Rigor mortis*…the progressive stiffening of the body that occurs several hours after death, it's caused by a chemical change in the muscles post-mortem. The body is decomposing slowly because of the chilly temperature in the room. All the windows were most likely purposely left open. She's been dead two days, tops. She was cut pretty deep. Looks like a butcher's job; the knife used was a really sharp one. I'll have more evidence for you when I get back to do an autopsy. The wood will be sent to the evidence room. Call Larry – he'll have information on it. My team is finished here; all we're waiting for is to take the body down."

Jones bent down to look at the two little spots on the floor in the dried blood.

"Brown, look at this. Is that an imprint?"

"It's not a handprint. What do you think it is?"

"Don't know, but I think we need to find out."

Jones looked around the room, saw a man with a camera, and got his attention.

"You…cameraman, take some pictures of this over here."

Jones focused his attention back on Torres and said, "Two days ago? So, that'll give us, what, Thursday or Friday?"

"In that time frame, yes."

"Ok…that's a start. Torres, stick around a bit. Let me and my partner take a look around, see what we can find, and I'll let you know when to bag and tag."

"Ok, Detective."

Brown looked at Jones and asked, "So, what do you think? Could be a ritual, or something domestic, or what?"

"Looks like a ritual…or something to that effect. Whoever did this took time to cut her up pretty bad, I'll tell you that much."

They took a little over an hour to search through all the rooms, trying to find clues. Jones came across an address book. One entry stuck out as clear as day: Mommy. They decided there was nothing else they could do at the crime scene. Jones called in C.S.U. to take down the body. Torres stood to the side, and Jones and Brown watched the men with New York City Morgue jackets come in. One man carried a stretcher, and the other man had a yellow and black Dewalt drill and a chair from the kitchen. The man with the drill stood on the chair and unscrewed the top of the cross, while the other kept the cross from falling down. Jones couldn't help but think that it probably took two people to put it up. Then, the man unscrewed the bottom one, and they laid the cross with the body still attached on the floor. They cut the leather straps, lifted the body, and placed it into a body bag. After they took it out, two other men carefully wrapped up the cross in plastic and also left.

Brown and Jones stayed around for awhile, talking to the residents to search for leads. They interviewed the landlord, but didn't really get much information. They also spoke to all of the tenants currently in the building, and made note of those who weren't home, so that someone could interview them later. The police sealed off the apartment, and they headed out to the address in the book, hoping to get some answers.

Chapter 6

NOTIFICATION OF THE DECEASED

The Flores residence was a renovated brick townhouse located among several other hundred thousand dollar townhouses in the Canarsie section of Brooklyn. Jones and Brown got out of the car, walked up the steps, and Brown knocked on the door. It was a few minutes before someone came.

"Hello. Can I help you?" an old, gray-haired man said when he opened the door.

"I'm Detective Jones, and this is my partner, Detective Brown. We're here to see Ms. Flores. Is she in?"

"Is this concerning Vanessa?"

"May I ask who you are?"

"Oh...I'm sorry, Detectives. I'm Vanessa's grandfather, Roberto Flores. Please come in. Valarie is right in here."

Ms. Valarie Flores sat in a leather recliner, facing the bay windows. There was a photo of the victim on a nearby end table. When she saw them come in, she immediately stood up.

"Hello, Ms. Flores?"

"Yes, I'm Ms. Flores. Who are you gentlemen?"

Jones said, "Ms. Flores, I'm Detective Jones and this is my partner, Detective Brown. There's no easy way to say this, but we found your daughter deceased in her apartment. We came to ask you some questions, and we'll need you to come make a positive identification."

Ms. Flores put her hands over her mouth to prevent herself from screaming. She stood staring at the detectives for a few moments. Then, she sat down, trying to digest what she'd just heard. Her eyes were turning red and swelling up, and she started crying uncontrollably. Jones sat next to her, put his arm around her shoulder, and was able to get her to calm down. But, before he could say anything, she said angrily, "It was her ex-boyfriend, Paul I know it. He always said he would kill her if she left him. He was very abusive towards my daughter, physically and emotionally."

Jones looked up at Brown, thinking of what he'd said back at the crime scene about a domestic dispute gone wrong.

"Are you sure you think he'd carry out that threat? You said his name was Paul?"

Brown took out his pen and pad and took notes.

"Yes, Paul Boyd, but my daughter always called him Paulie."

"Do you have a current address for him?"

"He's a bum. I don't know where he lives, but he hangs out and sells drugs in Brownsville…in those projects."

"Brownsville projects? I know the area. Do you happen to have a photo of him?"

"That's him next to her in that photo. You can have that, if you'd like."

Ms. Flores pointed to a photo that was on the mantle over the fireplace. Brown could smell charred wood as he reached over and took it down.

"Did she ever call the police and file a report?"

"I tried to get her to, but she wouldn't. I went down to the precinct myself to file a complaint, but I was told there was nothing the police could do without the victim coming in to file a report."

"That's normally what happens, but we'll pick him up for questioning. What did your daughter do for a living?"

"She worked as a waitress at a small café called Blue in Bedford Stuyvesant. That's where she met Paul. She worked there almost every night. She had to be there the night she was killed. He must have followed her home."

"Do you know of anyone else that would do this to her, other than Paul? Did she have any enemies?"

Ms. Flores used a tissue in her hands to wipe tears that were beginning to come again and said, "My daughter had no enemies, Detective. She was a good girl."

"Did she have any friends?"

"She has a best friend, Sharon Patterson. They were always together, and they both worked at the club."

"Do you have a number or address for her?"

"Yes, I'll go get it."

Ms. Flores went to retrieve the contact information, and Brown said, "Café Blue."

"You know the spot?"

"Yeah, I've been there before."

Ms. Flores came back with Sharon's number and address on a slip of paper and handed it to Jones.

"Thank you, Ms. Flores. We'll do everything in our power to catch the person or persons who did this."

Ms. Flores broke out crying again and grabbed Jones hands. He embraced her with open arms and said, "Everything is going to be all right, Ms. Flores."

Ms. Flores composed herself and said, "I'm sorry, Detective."

"Don't worry about it. "

"Thank you, Detective. I pray you find who did this."

"We will…are you up to coming to the morgue with us to identify the remains?"

"Yes, I am."

Her father said he wanted to come for support. Ms. Flores and Roberto got their coats, and they all headed to the morgue in the cruiser.

Chapter 7

—

MEDICAL EXAMINER'S OFFICE

Ms. Flores sat in a small waiting room, still wrapped up in her coat, gloves, and a blue wool hat. Roberto paced the room. Ms. Flores looked at the magazines on the table in front of her but didn't pick one up. Her hands were shaking and her mind wasn't really ready for what she was about to see. She wanted her daughter alive. Was the woman the police found her daughter, or had they made a mistake?

Jones and Brown walked down a long corridor and a set of stairs. Brown pushed through a set of double doors, and the smell of death was instantly evident. They walked into the morgue's examining room and saw Torres wearing a white lab coat and white scrubs. She stood looking at a body on a slab, writing into a folder. Brown couldn't help but notice her sexy, curvy body. Her glasses were tilted on the bridge of her nose. She put the folder down and picked up what looked like a heart out of a silvery oval pan. She stood and spoke to two pathologists, one of them pointed to the Detectives. Torres turned around.

Jones said, "Torres? Are we interrupting?"

She turned around and said, "No, Detectives, come right in. I have the body in here. The wood was sent to forensic for trace evidence, and they're looking into that as we speak."

They followed Torres over to another table. The silvery table looked cold and the body lying on it was pale, almost ghoul-like. The body was washed and the mutilation was clearer. The detectives could see how deep the cuts into the body of the victim really were.

Torres picked up a chart hanging on the side of the table. "She wasn't raped; there's no vaginal tearing. And I found no seminal fluid on her clothes, or on or in her body. I didn't find any blood on her clothes, either. I scraped her fingernails – nothing – and no drugs were found in her system." Flipping over to the next sheet of paper on the chart, she said, "She could have been killed first and mutilated after she was dead. Or mutilated first, and then killed. The killer used small leather straps to secure the victim's hands and legs. You see here, the straps were tight...cutting off blood circulation. That's why her hands look so puffy and dark. The killer then used a knife with a serrated blade to slit her throat and used it to cut ten inches into her body." Torres tilted the body to expose her back. "Here you see tiny holes in her skin. They were caused by small splinters that I pulled out of her back." She turned off the overhead light, picked up a forensic lamp, and went over the face of the corpse. "I found residue of chloroform around her mouth, and there were also small pieces of a white cloth in that area."

Jones said, "So, the killer used chloroform to render this woman helpless. There weren't any signs of a struggle inside the apartment. She must have been taken outside and brought inside. Torres, we have the victim's mother in the waiting room for identification."

"Say no more. I'll have her prepped and ready to view in twenty minutes. I've made a copy of the report. You can keep this file for your viewing."

Ms. Flores and Jones walked into the room first, with Roberto and Brown behind them. Ms. Flores was holding a tissue up to her eyes, trying to stop her flowing tears. Brown and Roberto stood to the side, while Jones walked with Ms. Flores to the steel slab. The white sheet covering the victim's body was smooth except for raised areas at her nose, feet, and breasts. Torres pulled down the sheet to reveal the victim's face. Ms. Flores started crying uncontrollably. She reached out her hand and grabbed Jones arm to keep from falling to the floor.

"Yes, that's my daughter." Ms Flores fell to her knees and grabbed at the sheet screaming, "Oh God, my baby, oh God my baby! Why, why?"

Roberto and Jones immediately took her back into the hallway with Brown following. They were able to calm her down just a little bit, but Jones knew the pain she was feeling would last a lifetime.

Chapter 8

THE 84ᵀᴴ

The Crown Vic rumbled as Jones and Brown pulled into their assigned parking spot at the precinct. They went into the building and were rushed by a wave of pure chaos… there was never a dull moment or boring day on the job. They made their way to the Captain's office and knocked on the door.

"Come in," the Captain said as he pointed to two seats in front of his desk while he held the phone to his ear. Brown and Jones took the seats and waited patiently as they watched the Captain go back and forth with whomever he was talking to. "Yes sir. We're working on it." "We have beefed up patrols around the city." - " The night shift usually…" – "Yes sir, you have a nice day also, and tell the wife I said hello." Jones looked at the name plaque on his desk: Captain Moore. He focused on a mental image of Captain Jones for a second, but he was a foot soldier. He loved the hunt and knew he would probably never give it up.

When Captain Moore was finished with his call, he hung up the phone and said intensely, "I just spoke with the Mayor. Inflation, taxes, and everything else is going up, and oh, of course, crime is also. I'm being pressured to bring crime down without the money to pay overtime. Bureaucratic bullshit, I think. But the rich somehow get richer and the hardworking man gets poorer. Anyway, gentlemen, what's the status with this case?"

Jones pulled out the crime scene pictures from the file Torres gave him and handed them to the captain. Captain Moore took them and started viewing them as he spoke. "This is definitely a case we need to keep on a need-to-know basis for the time being." Captain Moore's face cringed and his eyes opened wide as he looked at the photos. Each photo had a piece of paper attached to it with written detailed information on them.

Jones said, "We have a possible hit with the ex-boyfriend, a Paul Boyd, a.k.a. Paulie. The mother of the victim gave us a picture of him. She believes he killed her daughter. According to her, he was physically abusive and threatened to kill the victim if she left him."

"Do you like the ex-boyfriend for this?"

"Not sure until we talk to him."

"What else do you have?"

"We have a girlfriend of the victim, a Sharon Patterson. We'll question her to see if there's any information she can provide. Ms. Flores, the victim's mother, said they were always together. Also, the victim and Sharon Patterson worked at Café Blue, a club in Bedford Stuyvesant. We'll check that out and see what we find."

"What about prints?"

"We have hits… They're being processed now by Larry. We'll have something momentarily."

"Ok, get on the ex-boyfriend first. This just might end quickly. Do we know where he is?"

"The mother of the victim said he's in the Brownsville section of Brooklyn and that he's a low-level drug dealer. She didn't have a current address, but we'll check to see if we can come up with one. We have a recent photo of him. We'll pick him up and see what he has to say."

"Short version, what did the M.E tell you."

"The victim's been dead about two days. She wasn't raped, but she was tortured and cut up real bad. She also found traces of chloroform around the victim's mouth."

Captain Moore's eyes focused intently on the wood cross then flipped the photo and read the information on the paper. Then he handed the file back to Jones.

"Any information on the knife used and any evidence gathered from the wood?"

"We're going to stop by forensics right after we finish talking to you."

"Good work Detectives. Jones, I want you to take lead on this, ok? Do this right…no mistakes. After you two get on the ex-boyfriend, get to that club. Check to see if it has cameras. Talk to the bartenders; use a fine-toothed comb to handle this. I don't need to remind you two that we really need to get this guy. So keep on your toes, keep your ears and eyes open, and keep me informed. The last thing I need is the media involved."

After Jones and Brown left the captain's office they headed into the pit, "Jones, I'm going to go take a piss. I'll be right back."

"All right, I'll call the lab and see if they're ready for us to come down."

Jones picked up the phone, made the call, and Larry said he was ready for them. He hung up and read part of Torres' report to find out how the killer tore open the body. He tried to put himself in the killer's shoes. Why tear open the body? Why cut the victim's throat, why construct the cross-shaped wood, why make the body look as if it resembled Jesus Christ? He pulled out the pictures and tried to find something he'd probably missed at the crime scene. But he couldn't find anything. He came across the photo he'd told the photographer to take. He studied it closely; had he been kneeling in front of the body? He started to think so. His train of thought was broken by Brown as he sat down directly across from him at his desk.

"What's up, Jones? You got that look...you found something?" Brown said as he leaned back in his seat, his arms folded on his chest.

Jones held up the photo and pointed. "I'm trying to figure out what these spots are, here and here."

Brown took the photo. "I can't make it out either. Why, what are you thinking it could be?"

"I don't know, maybe Larry can give us an idea. He's ready for us in evidence. Maybe he can make something out of this."

—

Chapter 9

FORENSIC EVIDENCE

Larry was the smartest guy in the business; he could take anything apart and find a speck of blood under a foot of dirt. He could pull prints off just about anything, and the list went on. His long black hair and thick-rimmed glasses gave him an odd hippie-nerd look. Still, he was the man everybody came to, even other law enforcement agencies.

There were two parts of the evidence room. One area kept weapons used in crimes. Larry was the one who could easily tell you if a bullet in a crime came from the same gun and at what speed it was coming when it impacted. The other area of the room was full of computer equipment. Larry was also the best in computer forensics, and was working with images of the wooden cross on one of the computers when we entered.

"What's up, Larry? What do you have for us?"

"Ah…Detective Jones and Detective Brown."

Finishing up a tuna sandwich and wiping crumbs from his face, Larry stood up and walked over to the large piece of wood. "I've seen some crazy stuff in my time, but this cross is the craziest thing I've ever seen."

Brown said, "So, it definitely is a cross?"

"Yes, it is."

"We figured as much."

"I did an analysis of the wood...dogwood...don't know the whole story, but this type has some sort of religious connection."

Jones said, "Religious connection?"

"Yes, it has a reference to Jesus in some way, I'm sure."

"So, what else did you find?"

"Vertically, 84 inches, that's seven feet. Horizontally, it's 72 inches, which is six feet across. Both pieces are twenty inches wide all around. Total weight is sixty pounds. It was constructed to be easily assembled. You see this pin? I pull it forward, and both pieces can stand horizontally and be carried easily. These holes here were drilled in at each end and these leather straps carefully inserted."

Larry walked over to a table and pointed to the screws used to mount the cross on the wall. "These are 30-inch steel screws used for big construction jobs. The leather straps are five inches thick. I'd say you guys are looking for a carpenter killer of some sort. This piece is the work of a man that has knowledge of carpentry tools. By the way, the only DNA I found was the victim's. This is going to be a hard one to get, boys."

Jones said, "How many prints did you pick up in the apartment?"

"The team picked up three sets of prints throughout the apartment. One was the victim's, one was Paul..."

Jones interrupted him. "Let me guess: Paul Boyd?"

"How did you know?"

"The victim's mother gave him up."

"Well, the other one hasn't been identified, but I'm working on it. I'll have something soon."

Handing the photo to Larry, Jones said, "I want you to take a look at this photo and tell me what you see. I'm trying to figure out what these spots are."

"Let me take a look." Larry scanned the photo, pushed a few buttons, and it came up on a small screen.

"Ok, here's the picture you gave me on the right, and on the left is the high-resolution print. Now I'm going to magnify it and focus only on those spots you spoke of. Now, I really can't make out the top spots, but the lower spots look like the tip of toes. So I'm assuming these other spots have to be the knees."

Jones looked at Brown, and Brown moved a little closer to take a look at the picture and said, "So are we saying the killer was kneeling before the victim?"

Larry said, "From this view, I think that's exactly what the killer was doing."

"Any thoughts on why?"

"No clue."

Chapter 10

THE FIRST SUSPECT

Jones and Brown sat in the unmarked car, waiting to see if Paul Boyd would turn up. They were able to get a last known address for him, an apartment in the housing projects. They waited in front of a Chinese fast food place across the street from the projects, so they could observe the area first to see if they saw anyone who fit his description. They were able to match Ms. Flores' photo to information gathered from the police database.

After waiting for nearly three hours, they decided it was time to go in. There was a crowd of young black men in front of the building. When they saw the Detectives approach, they quickly started moving away. The Detectives grabbed the young men and put them up against the wall before they could run...Jones wasn't looking to chase anybody. He pulled the picture from his pocket of Paul Boyd and put it up to their faces to see if any of them matched.

"Brown, he's not here. I'll take the front entrance, and you take the back staircase."

"Ok."

Jones headed upstairs and was bombarded by the smell of urine. He stepped on several crack vials that littered the staircase. Once he hit the fourth floor, he pulled out his weapon and kept it to his side. Brown did the same, coming from the opposite side of the hallway. They stopped in front of apartment 4E. Brown put his ear to the door to see if he could hear anything, then knocked, hard.

"Police officers."

After twenty seconds, somebody opened the door, and Jones showed his badge. He opened the door wider until the inside door knob hit the wall and said, "We're looking for Paul. Is he here?"

A little, old black lady stood in front of them, scared and nervous at the same time. She glanced at their guns and knew whatever her grandson was involved in was serious. She put her hands in the pockets of her long, green nightgown. It took her a second to gather her thoughts.

"He's not here…what has he done now?"

Brown said, "We just have some questions to ask him, that's all. Do you mind if we check the residence?"

The lady seemed honest enough when she turned to look at Brown. Jones put his gun back into his holster but kept the safety off and the snap open, just in case. Brown cautiously did the same.

Jones repeated, "Do you mind if we check the residence?"

The old lady stood to the side and said, "Go ahead. He's not here."

Brown headed into the back, while Jones stayed with the old lady and kept an eye on the door, just in case their suspect entered.

"What's your name, ma'am?" he asked as he extended his hand.

"I'm Paul's grandmother. JoAnne Louis."

"I'm Detective Jones and that's my partner, Brown. When was the last time you saw Paul?"

"He was here this morning."

"Do you know what time he'll be back?"

"I don't know. He comes in at different times of the day and night. Did he do something bad?"

"No, ma'am, we just want to ask him a couple of questions, that's all."

Brown came back to the front and shook his head.

Jones said, "Ma'am, here's my card. Please have Paul call me as soon as possible when he comes in, ok?"

"Ok, I will."

They made their way downstairs and into the car. Brown started the car and they sat there for a second. Jones said, "We'll get him later. I really don't believe he did it anyway, but I still think it's a good idea we talk to him."

"What makes you believe he didn't do it?"

"This guy just doesn't fit the crime. I read his rap sheet; he's a petty crack dealer, never sold anything big, and hasn't done any real time. I just don't see it."

"Jones, this job tells us that anything is possible. Maybe he couldn't take it anymore and just tripped on her. Cut her throat and wanted to make a statement and put her on that wood and tortured her afterwards. So, are we going to sit here and wait to see if he shows?"

"Yeah, we might as well, at least for another hour or two."

"So tell me, what's up with you and Tamera, brother? You moved in."

"Yeah, I did it."

"Oh, she must have given you an ultimatum."

"It's not like that – I really love that woman. Listen, when you find the one, you'll know."

"I found her several times," Brown said as he started laughing.

"I don't mean it that way...look. Do you want to go the rest of your life being a playboy in the club? You wanna be fifty and trying to talk to young girls?"

"I'm still young...so I'm going to explore a little. Then, I'll find the right one and have her put pressure on me like Tamera put on you."

Jones watched Brown as he started laughing again.

"Whatever…Brown, you're not going to stay young forever."

They waited in front of the projects for hours to see if Paul was going to show up. Just as Brown was going to say something, someone knocked on their window and Jones rolled it down. "Yeah, what's up, Willie?"

Willie was one of the major street drug dealers in the neighborhood at one time, before he started getting high on his own supply. Now, he was just another lost soul caught up in the addiction, looking for a couple of bucks so he could get high. But even in his current condition, he was still a force to be reckoned with in the neighborhood.

"Yeah, man, I heard y'all looking for Paul Boyd. Maybe I could be of some help to you, you know."

Brown said, "Oh, yeah? How much is this going to cost us?"

"Y'all my people, so I'm thinking a bill would do it."

"I'll tell you what: I'll give you a fifty and promise not to haul your ass in to see if you have any outstanding warrants."

"You boys play hard…that'll work, though."

Brown reached in his pocket and said, "All I have is a twenty."

Jones felt in his pocket, pulled out a ten-dollar bill, and said, "Thirty dollars will have to do, Willie."

Willie reached in the car, took the money, folded it up, and put it in his pocket. He looked around and bent back down into the window opening.

"He's around the corner in the pool hall, been there all morning, drinking. I was in there not too long ago. He's still in there."

Brown pulled the car up in front of the poolroom and they could hear T-Pain's "I'm in Love with a Stripper" playing. Jones got out of the car, and Brown followed suit. They walked in and surveyed the room. The place was spacious; there stood three pool tables, a bar, and a dance floor. There were two big flat screens TVs, one behind the bar, and the other above the pool tables. And there he was: Paul Boyd, sitting down at the bar, talking to a woman. Jones took the right side of the room and Brown took the left. They walked right up to him; Paul didn't even realize what was going on until Brown called out his name.

"Paul. Paul Boyd?"

Paul turned around, he wanted to run, but there was nowhere to go, so he just sat there and played it cool.

"So, what can I do for you cops?"

"I'm Detective Jones, and this is my partner, Detective Brown. We want to ask you some questions about Vanessa Flores."

"Yeah…what about her?"

"We need you to come down to the precinct and answer some questions. It shouldn't take long."

Brown motioned for Paul to get up. Paul didn't move, didn't intend to until he got more answers.

"Answer what questions? I don't even fuck with that bitch anymore."

Jones was thinking either he was playing his role, or he didn't know she was dead. He grabbed his arm and said, "Watch your mouth, and let's go." He started to struggle with him a little, so he pushed him up against the bar and forced his head down to the counter, knocking over a can of beer. The liquid from the can spilled onto the floor. "We can make this hard or easy. Your choice." With Paul's head on the bar, it was hard for him to speak, but Jones wanted to make a strong impression and he did.

"Chill, man, all this isn't necessary."

Brown had his back; his hand resting on his gun, facing onlookers, some of the people in the club looked like they wanted to give Paul a hand.

"Get up quietly, and let's go have that conversation down at the station." Jones put the cuffs on him, grabbed the back of his neck, pulled him off the bar, and escorted him to the car with everybody in the poolroom watching. He sat in the back with him while Brown drove.

Chapter 11

—

THE INTERROGATION

A half an hour later, they arrived at the precinct. Jones handed Paul to a uniformed police officer, who put Paul in Interrogation Room One, which was furnished with a table and two chairs. Paul felt as if the bare beige walls were closing in on him. He looked up at the camera pointing down on him, took a look at the mirror- he knew it was a two-way.

Meanwhile, Jones and Brown discussed Paul's record with the Captain in another room. After an hour, they walked into the interrogation room. Jones pulled up a chair and laid a folder in front of him. Brown leaned up against the wall, and Jones started the questioning. Paul knew the routine. Good cop, bad cop.

"Can you tell me your whereabouts on the second of December?"

"Why?"

"Just answer the question."

"Why?" Paul said again. He bent down to look at the alcohol stains on his pants and his freshly wheat colored Timberlands from the bottle that was knocked down on the bar during the scuffle to put him in cuffs. He attempted to wipe it off, but the smell still lingered in close proximity. "You see this cop? All that fucking shit dripped down on my pants. I pay good money for my clothes."

"I'm a patient man, Paul, I am." Jones said as he pushed the folder to the side and put his feet on top of the table. "I'll tell you what. Downstairs, I have a whole cell full of individuals facing murder charges, never going to see freedom again. I'll just leave you in there with them for a couple of hours and maybe then you'll talk." Not that Paul was afraid, but did he really want to go through the hassle? Still showing signs of bravado, Paul said, "I was sitting at home, smoking a blunt."

"Oh, you think this is a joke?"

"Listen, police don't scare me. Y'all got the wrong cat for that. And it's the truth I was smoking a blunt."

"Paul, when was the last time you saw Vanessa?"

"About a week or so ago. What's this all about?"

"A week ago…what did you two talk about?"

Paul leaned back in his chair, its front legs in the air. "We just talked…look, if she said I hit her or anything like that… the bitch is lying."

Brown came off the wall, pushed Paul's chair upright, and said, "Answer my partner's questions, and don't be a smartass, asshole."

Paul put his hands on the table and folded them. "Ok, man, look, we talked…she wanted to break up. So I said 'see ya' and haven't heard or seen her since. What's the big deal with this?"

Jones opened the folder, threw the pictures of Vanessa's dead body on the table and spread them out so Paul could see them all. "I think the discussion went bad, and you killed her to make a statement. I also hear you were physical with her at times." Paul stood up and the chair he was sitting in fell to the floor, pointing his finger, defending his innocence he shouted. "Look, I smacked her around a bit, she was always getting on my fuckin' nerves, but this, you ain't gonna pin this shit on me."

Jones stood up and shouted, "Sit the fuck down now! Now, I'm going to ask you again: where were you on the second of December?" Brown came off the wall, and was going to tackle Paul onto the floor, but Jones shouted at Paul to pick the chair back up and to sit back down, so Brown backed off.

Knowing this was some real serious stuff; Paul was getting nervous and trying hard to remember that date. After a few seconds, he said, "I was at my grandmother's house all day playing Madden's video football game on Xbox Live. You can trace that shit. Then, I went out about nine and went over to this chick's house and spent the night there. You call her and my grandmother. Look, that chick got on my nerves, but I didn't want to kill her."

"Her mother thinks you did it."

"Her mother didn't like me at all from the start. And I never liked that bitch, but I didn't do this, I swear."

Then tears started to fall from his eyes.

Jones saw in his face he didn't do it, but checking his alibi was routine. He left the room with Brown following him.

"What do you think, Jones?"

"He didn't do it. I could tell in his face. A woman beater, yes, a drug dealer, yeah, but the way that woman was killed… no, he doesn't have it in him."

"Yeah, I agree."

Paul was kept in a holding cell for a few hours until the detectives could verify his alibi. It all turned out to be true, so they let him go, although Jones told him they might need to talk to him at a later date. Jones knew the first twenty-four hours were critical to solving the case, but at this point they had nothing. When Jones called Sharon Patterson, her answering machine picked up, so he left a detailed message.

Jones and Brown decided to take a ride over to Café Blue. They rode in silence, minds wandering, not really focusing on anything in particular. Brown broke the ice.

"You saw that dude went from hard to little girl in minutes."

They started laughing.

"Yeah, some of those guys really see the light when there's life or some real heavy numbers in front of them."

The car pulled up in front of a three story brick building with a huge sign that read "Café' Blue" hanging over the entrance.

Chapter 12

CAFÉ BLUE

The décor was old style Blues, it had an elegant and suave vibe Jones thought, photos of Blues legends all over the walls. The likes of B.B King, Muddy Waters, Little Walter, and others Jones or Brown didn't recognize. A group of five older black men were setting up band equipment. One of them stood setting up the microphone. Jones asked where the manager or owner was. The man pointed to the bar. The manager was an aging white fellow with an Irish accent, dressed in a cheap white suit, Brown thought, his hair short and all gray, he wore gold bracelets on each wrist. The Detectives interrupted the conversation he was having with a bartender; they showed him their badges and followed the manager to his office in the back.

The Detectives spent a little over two hours in the club, asking the manager questions and interviewing the bartenders and waitresses, but nothing sounded unusual. They got the surveillance footage and even were able to interview Sharon Patterson. So far they had nothing, so they headed back to the pit. There was nothing on the footage that stood out, even after watching it for four hours, winding and fast forwarding – nothing. Then, Jones cell phone rang. He looked at the caller I.D, saw it was Tamera, and answered. "What's up, baby?"

"Just called to see how your day is going."

"I've had better. I'm just finishing up here. What about you?"

"I'm on my way home now. Meet me there in a few?"

"I can't do that, but I'll meet you at home in about an hour or so, ok?"

"Ok, baby. I love you."

"Love you, too."

Jones hung up and Brown said, "I love you, baby...you sure she didn't whip it on you, brother?" Then he started laughing.

With a smirk on his face Jones said, "Look, let's wrap this up. There isn't much we can do here."

They walked into Captain Moore's office and told them their investigation into Paul Boyd was a dead end and Café Blue led them nowhere, also. They sat and talked about the case for thirty minutes. Captain Moore wasn't pleased with their investigation so far, but the case was still fresh. Something would surface soon. He gave them the o.k. to take off, but told them to keep their ears close to their mobile phones, just in case something popped up. Brown and Jones headed out to the car, and Brown, seeing that Jones was preoccupied, volunteered to drive.

On the way home, Jones couldn't help but think of the horrible crime. He had to solve this case. The pictures of the victim's body on that cross were disturbing. He just couldn't shake the view. He knew he probably wouldn't make good company tonight. Brown dropped him off in front of the building and honked the horn as he drove off. Jones waved him on and watched him as he continued to drive. He could still see the white cloud of smoke coming from the exhaust as Brown turned the corner.

Chapter 13

—

HOME SWEET HOME

Jones walked into the condo and was greeted with a big smile and a kiss. A man could get used to this, he thought. Oh, he'd had his reservations about moving in with Tamera, for sure. Living alone had its benefits: privacy, coming and going when you wanted to, different ladies coming by…but that got old, and coming home to an empty apartment started getting old, too. So, when he found The One, he went with it.

Tamera took his coat, hung it in the front closet, and said, "Glad you're home."

"I'm glad, too. Today was one of the craziest days in my career."

"Get relaxed. When you're finished, I'll be in the living room. I ordered some Chinese, ok?"

"Yeah, that'll work. Give me a minute to get myself together."

He looked at his watch and couldn't believe it was nine-thirty already. He went into the bedroom, changed his clothes, grabbed his laptop, and sat with Tamera in the living room.

Jones loved the place that was now also his: 650 square feet of luxury, plus a private balcony with a skyline view. An open chef's kitchen had top-of-the line appliances: a Viking stove, Subzero fridge, Bosch dishwasher, and wine cooler. Two elegant marble bathrooms had nice fixtures, deep-soak tubs, and separate glass showers. Oversized, soundproof windows let in lots of light and no noise. The nine-foot ceilings and hardwood floors were throughout the condo. There was enough space to live lavishly and entertain with ease, plus an enormous common courtyard, a terrace, a 24-hour doorman, full-service concierge, state-of-the-art fitness center, private underground garage, refrigerated storage room for Fresh Direct deliveries, and complimentary shuttle service to and from the subways. But what he liked most was the 52" inch Samsung flat screen in the living room area.

He settled into the end of the brown leather sectional sofa and caught Tamera smiling at him. He blew a kiss and she pretended to grab it. She smiled again and continued to eat. They ate and talked, then went into their little worlds. Tamera was working on her book, typing on her Gateway laptop, and Jones went searching for answers on his Toshiba laptop. He brought up Google and searched for information on dogwood. He wanted to know if it had any significance in the case – he was sure it did, somehow.

Jones was soaking in the information; he read there were debates about the wood used to build the cross on which Jesus was crucified. There were some who believed the cross was made of olive wood or cedar. Others suggested perhaps it was cypress or plane tree wood. Some even suggested dogwood was used, but there weren't any biblical references to the dogwood tree. There were different types of dogwood; the pink dogwood was said to be blushing for shame because of the cruel purpose, which it served in the crucifixion. The weeping dogwood further symbolized the sorrow. The red dogwood, called the Cherokee, bore the color to serve as a remembrance of Christ.

Looking for the information made him question his own belief in Christianity. He was brought up to believe in God and still called His name when in need, but questioned His reality because of the horrible things he'd seen. Thinking about the case made him question it even more. He wondered if there truly was a God, why would He let something like this happen to Vanessa Flores?

He took the opportunity to research more on the subject of Jesus Christ. His knowledge of Christianity was limited, and to solve a case like this, he wanted to know all he could absorb. He also needed to know who sold dogwood lumber.

The search led into the night. He tapped on keys, read and read, and before he knew it, he was fast asleep. Tamera also stayed up, typing and typing. When she looked over and saw Jones asleep, she held her hand up to her mouth, yawned, and decided it was time for her to turn in. She grabbed a blanket and lay beside him.

Chapter 14

ANOTHER MURDER/TUESDAY MORNING

"Damn, it's freezing this morning, and there are still piles of snow all over the city. The city never sleeps, and it looks like the city workers aren't doing their jobs. On the way here I saw two snow plows just sitting, where were the drivers? Who knows". Brown said as Jones got in the car. He only caught part of what Brown was saying. He was deep in thought about the hours that had passed and still nothing… nobody knew anything.

Brown and Jordan walked into the pit, ready to get to work with no leads at all. They both thought the case would end up unsolved. Jordan sat at his desk, while Brown went to get a cup of coffee. He started looking over messages he had, trying to decide who to call back first. Then, his phone rang.

"Hello, Detective Jones speaking."

"Hello, Detective. It's Sergeant Morrison. I thought I'd let you know we just got a call. It seems we have another murder like the one you're investigating. Wright, Johnson and I are getting ready to go out right now."

"What's the location?"

"877 Green Street, not far from the first victim."

Brown came back with two cups of coffee and knew something was up when he saw the expression on Jones' face. "What's going on?"

Jones got up and put on his coat. "I just got a call from Sergeant Morrison. There's another murder, same M.O."

Brown passed a cup of coffee to Jones, and he took it. They went into the Captain's office and informed him that there was another murder and that it might be the same killer. The Captain grabbed his coat, and they all left the pit for a waiting police cruiser out front. Jones was betting the Captain's interest wasn't because of the fact that there was another body, but looking good for political gain.

They rode in silence and were greeted by Officer Wright when they pulled up at the scene.

"The body's on the third floor," Officer Wright said as he escorted the Captain, Brown, and Jones into the building.

The Captain asked, "Is C.S.U. on the scene?"

"No, sir, not yet."

Jones asked, "Any witnesses so far?"

"No, sir, but officers are checking with everyone in the building."

They walked into the apartment and were directed to the living room. When they saw it was a dead woman on a cross,

Jones knew the same person who had killed Vanessa Flores had killed this woman.

Brown and Jones walked over to the body, while Captain Moore went to talk to Sergeant Morrison and the first officer on the scene. Jones said "thank you" for the heads up to the Sergeant before Captain Moore pulled him to the side. Jones thought the last thing they needed now was for too many people to be on this case at the same time. Jones pulled Captain Moore to the side when he finished talking and told him that they needed Torres on the scene. She was already aware of the last case and could be trusted to keep quiet. Captain Moore made a call, and Jones gave Torres a call and briefly explained the situation. From this point on, she would be lead crime scene investigator. Brown and Jones observed the body and didn't touch anything. They didn't want to contaminate the scene. Brown, though, was looking at the woman intently like he seen a ghost.

Jones asked, "Brown, what is it?"

"I've seen her before."

"You have?"

"Yes…I remember now…Saturday, a lady came in saying her daughter was missing, and I can swear this is the girl in the picture she showed me. Wait, let me think… elderly woman…and she said her name was…Ms. Jackie Washington."

"Are you sure?"

"I'm positive. I left the photo and her information in my desk, but there should be a missing ten-fifty-seven report with her name on it."

Jones bent down to look at the blood on the floor and saw the same type of impressions that he'd seen at the other crime scene. This killing was identical in every way, from the strapping of the body to the mutilation. The room was cold, cold enough that like the first body the detectives saw, the killer kept the body well preserved, statue like, frozen in time. Was that what the killer wanted? A statue of death. Was this supposed to be god-like, a replica of Jesus on the cross?

The room was filled with crime scene personnel assisting Torres, poking and prodding at the dead body, taking photos, measuring the length of the body, focusing on the straps used to bind the body to the wood. Torres stood still, her forensic kit open, gloves on, she focused her hands on the mutilation, and one word crossed her mind- horrifying. Her assistants dusted for prints and searched the apartment for possible murder weapons or the weapon itself. Jones and Brown also searched the apartment making sure they didn't interrupt anyone doing their job. Just like the other apartment, nothing was found, no evidence, the killer left nothing but the dead.

Chapter 15

—

POLITICAL GAIN

Captain Moore sat at his desk looking over the case files of the two murders. His eyebrows lifted and his pupils were fixed on the photos of the dead women. The torture these women endured at the hands of a monster was something he wouldn't want to happen to anybody. And yet it did. The cross was unsettling to him, why would anyone mark the death of Jesus? He knew his job was far less interesting than the job his detectives had of solving the case, of a cross killer. He knew Jones and Brown were good police officers, but detectives, he didn't know, this being Jones' first big case and Brown's second. Captain Moore put down the case files and searched his desk drawers for Jones and Brown's jackets. He was thinking of taking them off the case and assigning more experienced detectives, knowing it would look like an inexperienced move on his part, but thought it may be necessary for a case of such magnitude. He knew if they were to solve the biggest case in New York City it would make them heroes and make him look pretty good. He saw an opportunity to run for mayor, or chief of police. He knew the Mayor well enough to be chief of police, and he knew he would have the backing of the Police Association and other important people that would support his campaign for mayor. Decisions, decisions, he thought. When the time came he would know and make his move.

The radiator made rumbling noises and shook as the heat filled the room in spurts. Captain Moore walked over to it and kicked the lower part of it, and the noise and shaking stopped. The building was old and needed renovation but again the city said no money was available for over-time, replacements of old and used equipment, so how were the police agencies able to do their jobs, Captain Moore thought.

Captain Moore sat reading over Jones' jacket, first a 10-71 shooting, the case of a man he killed interested him the most, Jones was a beat cop with three years on the force at the time.

1700 hrs I was 10-10 off duty. I just dropped off my girl-friend at home and was headed home myself. I stopped by a Super Fresh to pick up some milk and a box of Captain Crunch for breakfast for the following morning. When I came out of the store carrying my bag, I heard two men arguing. I continued to my car and got in. The two men were visible, but I didn't see a need to get involved until there were several gunshots fired. I ducked behind the dashboard and put my hand under the passenger seat and grabbed my licensed Berretta Bobcat. I kept the gun in my car just in case. When I emerged from under the dashboard I saw a black male standing over a man lying on the ground. The man raised his gun again and was going to shoot the man again. I exited the car with my gun drawn. Following procedure I identified myself as a police officer.

Word by word, Captain Moore was impressed by Jones' way of detailing the whole incident. His grammar, punctuation, and his writing skills were good. Captain Moore had read a lot of case files; officers using misspelled words, sentences that he had to mentally fill in to understand what was being written, but this report was as if he were reading a book.

The assailant raised his gun and took a shot at me. I quickly took cover behind my car. The bullet just missed me by inches. The assailant took another shot at me and the bullet struck my car window shattering it. The sound of the glass shattering sounded like a small explosion to my ears.

Dramatic, Captain Moore thought.

Then the assailant took off running, knocking people out of the way as he ran. I came from behind my car and gave chase after him but not before I showed my badge and yelled to the store clerk, who came outside to see what was going on, to call the police and call an ambulance. I followed the man as he entered an alleyway. He took another shot at me. I ducked and was able to avoid the bullet. I again identified myself as a police officer but the man wouldn't stop. We ended up two blocks away. I took cover in a doorway while the assailant took cover behind a red Honda Accord. The assailant took two more shots at me hitting the edge of the doorway, breaking off small pieces of concrete and wood near my face. People were running and ducking everywhere, trying not to get caught in the crossfire. I ducked in the doorway a little more, trying not to get hit, and then I took four shots at the assailant as he stood up to shoot at me again. I hit him all four times-once in the neck, twice in the chest and once in the right shoulder. He stumbled backwards shooting wildly up in the air as he fell to the ground. Then there was a thud, then silence. I came out from the doorway holding my gun in both hands pointing straight ahead until I came up to the shooter. I kicked the man's gun away, bent down to check his pulse, there was none, he was dead.

After reading Jones' report, Captain Moore was comfortable with him being the forerunner in the cross killings case. Captain Moore pulled out Brown's jacket; he flipped through the sheets of paper in the folder that lay atop his desk. He was looking for the file containing the information that brought Brown to his unit. He found it, leaned back in his chair and started reading.

I stood in an empty apartment with only a kitchen table. I stood looking out the window on the first floor of a three-story apartment building. I was using police-issued binoculars, keeping an eye on my partner, detective Harold Croft badge num# 4567. My partner, after two years under cover, made his way into a small group of skin heads bringing in large quantities of cocaine and guns. I was brought in undercover, after Harold infiltrated the group, to watch his back. He was to make a huge transaction, money for drugs, and money for guns; I guarded fifty two thousand dollars, the currency being used for four kilos of cocaine, and ten thousand dollars for over twenty ak-47s. I watched as detective Croft came walking back to the building using his hidden microphone to convey the deal was about to go down.

Once my partner entered the apartment we waited for the arrival of the men to make the transaction. Two bald headed white men walked in, both wearing green army fatigues. There was a brief commotion of my being there with Harold and that I was black. Harold defused the conversation quickly and we proceeded to do business. Harold asked to see the weapons and drugs.

The taller of the two perps put a red and black duffle bag on the floor and took out a p-90, a Belgian designed submachine gun equipped with a silencer. The man pointed the submachine gun at me and my partner while his partner pulled out another one from the bag. The taller perp demanded that I kick over the bag of money. Harold engaged in conversation until he was told to shut up. I kicked the bag complying with the demand. The other perp grabbed the bag and opened it. He reached in and took out a stack of marked hundred dollars bills. He took a step back and the other perp started shooting, striking my partner Harold Croft first, hitting him multiple times. I took out my police-issued Glock nine millimeter and started shooting. Hitting the shooter in the shoulder and I took cover behind one of two tables in the room. The man I shot hit the floor, dropped the weapon and stopped moving; his partner took the weapon off the floor and started shooting both p-90s wildly at the table. I reached my hand over the table and started shooting in an attempt to push the attacker back. He kept shooting, I gave the go code and two flash grenades crashed into the window and exploded, blinding the perp. The squad entered the apartment and we were able to gain control of the situation.

Captain Moore didn't read it all because he knew the rest, Brown's partner that night, Harold Croft, died- a sad day for the police department and his friends and family. One of the perps died and the other was sent away for life. Making a decision to take the detectives off the case wasn't an option, it was their hit, so they'll see it through. He put the folders back, got up and took his coat from the rack, put it on and exited the building. As he was getting into his car, his cell phone rang. It was an old friend, Cheryl Muhammad.

Chapter 16

—

FINGERPRINTS

Informing Ms. Jackie Washington in person about what happened to her daughter, Pamela, left an uneasy feeling inside Jones as he sat at his desk. Detectives Jones and Brown watched Ms. Washington go straight into cardiac arrest in front their eyes. After the medics took her away, they sat in silence for a while.

Sitting at his desk, Jones took the time to read over the files of Vanessa and Pamela's murders, trying to focus on what was written in Torres' reports and his notes. He took the pictures of the bodies out and pinned them on a board behind his desk. He got on his computer and searched criminal files, trying to find killers with this pattern, but couldn't find any. A new psycho had emerged, and he's a mean son of a bitch.

Jones stood up and addressed Brown. "What are we not seeing? We have two killings by the same person. Larry confirms this dogwood was used in both killings. So, it plays a significant role in both cases. He couldn't find any hairs, fibers, fingerprints…nothing. I did some Internet searching the other night and found out something interesting about the wood."

"The wood?"

"Yeah, go with me on this for a second. There are several people that believe that Jesus was crucified on this type of wood. The killer has killed twice already, same everything."

"So, we're dealing with a serial killer?"

"Maybe…Brown, look at this picture. It's almost identical to this one. I'm thinking before or after the killer murders his victims, he prays or something. Maybe he's sacrificing these women."

"Sacrificing…praying…this sounds crazy, Jones."

"These murders are crazy."

"You got a point there."

"Look, we need to start looking at who has this type of wood, and we'll get a little closer to whoever killed these two women. I'll call Larry and have him get on this."

Their conversation was interrupted by Jones' desk phone.

"Give me a second – let me answer this. Homicide, Detective Jones speaking."

"Jones, it's me, Larry. I got something that might just help you two. It's a long shot, but it's something."

"I was just about to call you…what you got?"

"I got a hit on that other print on the Flores case."

"Good. Whose is it?"

"The landlord's."

"The landlord...why wouldn't his print be in the house? He's the landlord."

"On the dresser in the woman's bedroom...now, why would his fingerprints be there?"

"Ok, I'm listening."

"I found a case file on Franklin Jefferson from over twenty years ago, but get this: his real name is Franklin Thomas. He changed it when he was twenty-one. He was charged with domestic assault and attempted murder. I had a look at the photos of the woman involved in that case twenty years ago...brutal. He pleaded it down to domestic assault. He wasn't charged as an adult. His prints were taken, but because he was a juvenile, they were never processed with the file, and when he was released, the file was closed. I emailed you the file I.D. number, so go take a look."

"So, how did you come to look for it?"

"I checked juvenile files and came up with a hit."

"Ok, did the crime scene unit find his prints at the Washington murder?"

"No, but..."

Jones interrupted him before he could finish. "Good work, Larry, we'll get on it. I have something I want you to check out."

"What is it?"

"I need you to see who distributes, carries, or has anything to do with dogwood lumber."

"I'll get right on it."

Jones hung up the phone and thought for a second before he told Brown of Larry's findings. Finding Mr. Jefferson's prints at the Flores murder scene hardly made him a suspect, but at this point, it was worth looking into.

"Larry got a hit in the Flores killing. The landlord's print was found on the victim's dresser. He was charged with domestic assault and attempted murder some years ago, but pleaded it down to domestic assault. Larry said it was brutal. Apparently, he changed his last name from Thomas to Jefferson. Maybe we should pick him up in the morning. I'll print out the file so we can look it over."

Jones got on the computer and was able to pull the file from the number Larry had emailed him. He printed two copies of the report and handed one to Brown. After reading the files, they both thought it was a good idea to bring in Mr. Jefferson. Jones took it a little farther by having Captain Moore get a judge to sign a search warrant for Mr. Jefferson's apartment at seven o'clock that evening.

When Captain Moore called him almost three hours later, he told him that they were basically going on a hunch. The captain said he'd explained to the judge the violent nature of Mr. Jefferson's assault on his victim. That was enough to give them a warrant to check his apartment. Their main focus was to find the murder weapon.

Jones hung up the phone and said, "We have a warrant to check the premises."

"In the morning?"

"Catching him early in the morning sounds good."

Jones sat in his chair and waved at Brown as he walked out of the pit. Jones stayed behind thinking about Mr. Jefferson. Fumbling with a number two pencil, thinking out loud, "Whoever killed these women was definitely somebody who'd lost his marbles." His train of thought was broken by the phone ringing.

"Hello, Detective Jones. How can I help you?"

"It's me, Jordan."

"Hey, baby. How did your book signing go tonight?"

"Good…sold a lot of books."

"That's good news. I'm so proud of you."

"Why, thank you. I try," Tamera said, laughing. "You haven't forgotten about tomorrow night, have you?"

Leaning back in his chair, placing the pencil on his desk, holding the phone to his ear, he answered, "No, I didn't forget we're going to Delaware."

"Ok, I'll see you tonight. Try not to stay in your office all night, ok?"

"So, what time are we getting ready tomorrow?"

"About five."

"Ok, I'll be ready then. I'll be done in a few, so I'll see you soon."

Chapter 17

—

WARRANT

Wednesday morning Jones didn't waste any time once the warrant came through the fax; they headed straight for the Jefferson residence. They arrived at the apartment building at 5:45 in the morning, and Jones knocked on the door moments later. When Mr. Jefferson answered, he found detective Jones standing in the doorway with his game face on and his badge at his eye level. He had the warrant in his left hand and his right hand was leaning on his weapon, with the holster open.

"Mr. Jefferson, we have a warrant to check your residence." Dressed in an all blue pajama pants set covered over by a dark blue housecoat, with black slippers on, Mr. Jefferson answered.

"What is this all about?" Mr. Jefferson said, scratching his head in confusion.

Brown wasn't much for explaining; pushing Mr. Jefferson aside he led a team of uniformed police officers inside the apartment and started the search.

"You didn't tell us about your brush with the law, Mr. Jefferson."

"What are you talking about?" Mr. Jefferson said as he grabbed the piece of paper out of Jones hand and started reading it.

"Mr. Jefferson, you're welcome to watch my men and partner search your dwelling or wait in a police cruiser."

"I think I will... wait a second here do you think I killed that woman?"

"You'll have a chance to explain your past criminal history and ask questions later at the precinct. Wright, Johnson, keep Mr. Jefferson company while I join the search."

Ironically, the opening musical notes of *The Jeffersons* were playing on a small color TV resting on a black and white TV stand. Jones entered the apartment and watched as one police officer searched through a bookcase on the left side of the wall. Two more officers were lifting pillows from the couches in the living room area. He went further into the apartment and found Brown in the kitchen, opening cupboards and pulling out dishes and cups. Then, he opened up the utensils drawer and took out all the knives, passing them off to another officer, who started bagging them as the possible murder weapon. Jones walked into the bedroom, which the last officer was pulling apart. It looked as if a tornado had come through, leaving nobody alive.

Nothing that they found would indicate Mr. Jefferson was the person of interest, but that didn't mean he wasn't.

Wright and Johnson escorted Mr. Jefferson to the precinct, while Jones and Brown dropped off the knives at Larry's lab and headed to the interrogation room.

Chapter 18

—

EIGHTY-FOURTH PRECINCT

Jones and Brown stood looking at Mr. Jefferson through the two-way mirror. They were both holding Dunkin' Donuts cups of coffee, taking sips at almost the same time. Brown said,

"He doesn't look like much of a crazed killer on a killing spree."

"Ted Bundy didn't either."

"You have a point there."

Mr. Jefferson sat patiently for thirty minutes, waiting for whoever was coming to speak to him, until he grew impatient. He stood up, walked over to the mirror, and used his hands to smooth down his freshly cut hair, unaware that he was being watched. With every stroke, he admired his side waves of salt and pepper hair and beard. He observed his clothes, a dark blue sweater and a pair of black khakis, in the mirror. He'd put on the first thing he could find before being rushed downtown for questioning by the police so early in the morning. He'd asked why they thought he had anything to do with Vanessa Flores' murder, but they refused to answer him. He licked his thumb, bent down, and tried to wipe a scuffmark off one of his black shoes. He stood back up and walked around the room.

Opening up the folder of Mr. Jefferson's case from years ago, Jones said, "Like you said before Brown, you never can tell these days, right? This is still a lead worth looking into. You ready?"

"I'm ready."

"Let's do it."

Mr. Jefferson continued to walk around the room, looking at nothing in particular, but stopped when the door opened.

"Have a seat, Mr. Jefferson," Jones said as he walked into the room. He sat down directly across from where Mr. Jefferson had been sitting.

"So you think I killed that woman," Mr. Jefferson said as he sat down. "Do I need to call a lawyer?"

"Do you think you need a lawyer?"

"You tell me, if I'm being accused of killing that woman… then yes, I might need one."

"Did you kill her?"

"No."

"Then you don't need a lawyer." Mr. Jefferson sat quietly; he wanted to bring it down a notch, he was after all being questioned in reference to a murder, and he didn't want to make things worse. Cooperate, he thought.

Brown walked into the room and leaned up against the wall with his arms folded. His gaze never left Mr. Jefferson; he was looking for a weakness.

Jones said, "Want a cup of coffee or something?"

"No...no thanks."

"Let's go over your statement you gave the police. You said you went to the apartment because neighbors reported a foul smell coming from it."

Mr. Jefferson sat up in his chair, eager to help the police in any way he could. "Yes, I got the complaint about two days before I actually went over there."

"So when was the last time you saw the victim?"

"Umm...about two weeks ago. She called me to come over and fix her dresser."

Jones knew that his answer was sincere; he could hear it in his voice. Larry had said Mr. Jefferson's prints were on the dresser. That question was answered, but he wasn't convinced yet, so he pushed on.

"Are you a Christian, Mr. Jefferson?"

"What?"

"Are you a Christian?"

Mr. Jefferson sighed, and shrugged but answered the question. "I guess...I haven't been to church in years, though. What is this, where is this going?"

"Ok, I'll just go right into it. Under the name Frank Thomas, you committed a crime in 1988, a very violent assault against your then girlfriend."

Mr. Jefferson got closer to the table and folded his hands on top of it.

"Don't tell me you think I killed that woman."

"Why did you kill her?"

"I didn't. I didn't, I didn't." Mr. Jefferson slammed his fist on the table.

"But you almost killed your girlfriend twenty years ago...and you changed your name...why?"

Mr. Jefferson got a little aggressive. "This is bull shit that was a long time ago. I just lost control – no big deal."

Standing up, Detective Jones placed his hands on the table and raised his voice a little bit,

"No big deal...so, you lost control with Vanessa because she didn't want to...want to give you some, you know have sex."

Mr. Jefferson stood up.

Brown came off the wall. "Have a seat, Mr. Jefferson. Right now," he commanded, pointing his finger at him. His stance was strong and his voice was authoritative.

Mr. Jefferson looked at Brown, took a seat, and then focused on Detective Jones again.

Detective Jones voice a little louder, he repeated, "Now, again, why did you change your name?"

Mr. Jefferson slouched in his seat…he already knew this was serious, but knowing he had nothing to with this murder put him on edge. Not wanting to be a scapegoat for this murder ran through his mind. He didn't want to show any signs that he was guilty, but being nervous was something he couldn't help. They wanted him for this, maybe; he was confused and the pressure was making him jittery. He sat up in his chair and spoke as calmly as possible, but it was obvious he was shaken up.

"I changed my name because my parents thought it would be a good idea, so they made it happen. I was young and dumb, doing drugs. I went by my old lady's house, we got into an argument, and it got a little rough."

"A little rough?" Jones yelled and threw the photos of the first victim's dead, mutilated body on the table with enough force that they scattered, showing all twenty-two of them.

Raising his voice, "You killed her, you killed this woman. Why?"

"Look, why are you doing this?" Mr. Jefferson said as his eyes started to get watery. He quickly wiped his face.

The detectives both looked at the expression on Mr. Jefferson's face: an expression of shock. Was this the first time he'd seen this particular scene? The first time he'd seen a person dead? Jones didn't want the expression on

Mr. Jefferson's face to divert him from questioning the suspect, so he pushed on.

"I'm trying to catch a killer, Mr. Jefferson, that's why, and every rock has to be overturned."

"I didn't do this, Detective, I didn't."

"Do you think I was born yesterday, sir? You killed this woman. Make it easier on yourself, and tell me what happened. Then, maybe I can help you."

"I didn't do this, I didn't do this."

Jones really knew at that point Mr. Jefferson wasn't their killer, but the case was getting to him. He knew it, and most importantly, he didn't want to cross the line between his personal feelings and the law. He put the pictures back in the folder, but couldn't get the images out of his mind. He wiped his face, gathered his thoughts. "Mr. Jefferson, I want to thank you for your cooperation. You've been very helpful. If I have any more questions, someone from my office will contact you."

Detective Jones got up and left the room with Brown following him.

"Jones, you all right?"

Brown had never seen him take a case personally, but this case was different and he could tell this one had him. The detectives had solved over ten cases since becoming partners. All the cases were quick arrests: boyfriend kills girlfriend, robber kills store clerk—crimes of that nature. The results, indictments, eight out of ten of them were convicted and sentenced to hard time. This case however was nothing like the rest; this case was something out of a movie script that made its way into reality. The pressure was building and Brown knew Jones being lead detective on the case had brought on a whole new headache.

"Yeah, I'm ok. Have Johnson and Wright take him where he wants to go. I'm going to take a breather for a second. I'll be at my desk."

Jones sat at his desk and leaned back in his chair. He hadn't gotten much sleep last night. He stayed up most of the night, listening to Tamera talk about her book signing. Brown came back and sat at his desk, picked up the receiver, dialed a number, and started talking. Jones listened to him for a second and knew he was deep in conversation with one of his many women. Listening to his slick talk sometimes amused him. Did women really go for that pimp talk?

Smiling, closing his eyes for a second, the images of the dead women were there again, haunting him. For the first time in his career, Detective Jones found himself constantly thinking about a case on and off the job. He'd never had so much trouble solving a case before. What was he missing?

His line was ringing, and Brown noticed Jones was in another place, something else he had never done before. Jones was always on point, so he knew this case was definitely getting to him. Brown told his female friend to hold, and he answered his line.

"Detective Brown. How can I help you?"

"Hi, Maxwell, how are you?"

"I'm fine, Tamera. How are you?"

"I'm doing well. Is Jordan there?"

"He's right here – hold on a sec."

Brown held down the phone and covered the mouthpiece so Tamera couldn't hear.

"Jones…Jones…Jones?"

"Yeah?"

"You ok?"

"Yeah, just thinking. What's up?"

"Tamera's on the line for you."

"Ok, transfer it."

Brown hit transfer and clicked back over to his conversation.

Jones sat up and pressed the flashing button. "Hey, baby, what's up?"

"I'm doing ok. How's your day going?"

"So far, it's okay. So, what are you doing?"

"I just loaded three boxes of books into my car, picked up my outfit, and I'm about to get some lunch. I'm famished.

Will you be home by five? We need to leave early enough for the drive out to Delaware."

"I will…and I look forward to my baby doing her thing tonight."

"I also got you an outfit. Hope you don't mind."

"No…you have good taste. I would've done a bang-up job at that because you know I suck at that type of thing."

They both started laughing.

"So I'll be home in a few hours, just going to finish up here, ok?"

"Ok. See you later."

Chapter 19

—

MAXWELL AND TORRES

Brown was dressed to impress, wearing a Claiborne grey pinstripe suit, and was standing looking into the full length mirror, "Damn, I look good," he said out loud. He grabbed his keys to the rental. He was outside his apartment building standing in front of the Jaguar, pulling out his cell phone he called his date. "Hello?"

"Hello, it's me Maxwell."

"Hello. And how are you?"

"I'm doing well, how are you?"

"I'm getting ready- almost done. You can come pick me up. I should be ready by the time you get here."

"Ok, I'm on my way, see you in a few." Brown closed the flip on his Samsung and entered the vehicle. Nice, he thought. He wanted to rent something sexy, something that would leave a good impression. He started the car and pulled out into the street. He never dated anyone like Torres; she was different, sexy, smart and someone who he could take home to momma. Jones was doing well with Tamera; maybe it was time for him to make a move also, he thought. He pulled up in front of the house located in Spanish Harlem. The Jag shining, he got out, walking up three steps he stood on the porch and rang the bell. Carrying flowers he bought earlier, still with that fresh flowery smell, someone opened the door. "Hello, Maxwell."

Brown was taken aback; he was used to seeing Torres in uniform but seeing her in the dress she wore tonight made Brown feel like he hit pay dirt. The blue dress clung to her in a way that showed every curve on her body.

"Hello. These are for you." Torres could see the shiny watch on his left wrist and was impressed with the flowers and the suit Brown had on. Dapper, she thought.

Smelling the flowers she said, "Thank you. Come in and have a seat." Torres held the door open and took the flowers. Walking over to a stand near the front window, Torres sat the flowers down. Picking up a leather jacket, Brown grabbed hold to it and said, "Here, let me."

"Oh, you're good."

"What? Just being a gentleman."

Brown held the jacket as Torres slipped her arms into it and opened the door for her. They walked onto the porch and Torres locked her door. Brown was already at the Jag with the passenger door open. "Oh, you're real good, Mr. Brown." Brown smiled, closed the door, got into the Jag and drove off. "So, where are we going?"

"A special place, for a special person."

The Jag pulled up to a well-known restaurant- Bello Giardino, located in the Upper West Side of Manhattan. Parking was something of a nightmare in Manhattan, day or night, it didn't matter; Brown covered all the basics and didn't mind paying the extra dollar to make a good impression- valet parking. The valet, dressed in a black suit, came running over to them. As Brown exited the car, the valet opened the passenger door, and Torres with all her elegance exited, welcoming the service. Not long after the Jaguar sped away and Brown put the stub in his pants pocket, the doorman opened the door and Brown and Torres entered the restaurant-instant service. Walking over to them, a hostess introduced herself and escorted them to their table that was already reserved. Handing them menus, the waitress said, "Would you two like anything to drink?" Brown said, "I'll have a Corona." Torres said, "I'll have a glass of water." The waitress hurried off. Putting down her menu, Torres said, "This is a nice place, Brown."

Unbuttoning his jacket, Brown said, "Thank you, only the best for you."

"Oh, you're too smooth."

Brown started laughing and said, "Anything you like? The food on the menu looks great."

"I'm thinking." The waiter came back with their drinks. She sat the tray down and took the water and bottle of

Corona off the tray and set it on the table. "Are you two ready to order?" Brown ordered the traditional Spaghetti and Meatballs and Torres ordered Chicken Parmigiana.

The food came and Brown and Torres dug in. Torres took a look around the place and loved the decor, real fancy, she thought. They were escorted to a table near the window, and the view wasn't bad; it mixed in very well with the mood. Torres was twenty-three; she spent most of her life in school, one boyfriend in her life that never went anywhere. Her mother always said to be careful when looking because, when you look, you always get the opposite, and that's what happened. She wasn't looking this time. Brown found her, and she liked him, but still kept her guard up. "Has this case bothered you any, lately?" Torres said, as she pushed aside her drink.

"Bothered? Well it is a case that screams, 'I'll need to see a therapist' after viewing the bodies. I guess you can say that, yes a little. What about you?"

"I'm used to seeing dead bodies all the time" Torres was lying, she saw maybe ten or thirteen bodies in her career but Brown didn't know that. "It's what I do, but this is, this is a little different from what I'm used to seeing. I usually get gunshot victims, car crash victims, never have I ever came across a body mutilated deliberately."

"I figured you see stuff like that all the time. How long have you been a medical examiner?"

"A year and a half."

"Well, don't feel bad. It's my first serial killer."

"Any leads yet?"

"Not yet, but we're looking into a lot of things, the cross...disturbing."

"To say the least."

"We still haven't determined if this is religious or not. Our first suspect, Paul Boyd, wasn't much of the bad boy he plays on the street. He was a suspect in the Vanessa Flores murder. The victim's mother led me and Jones to him. Turns out he's a big baby, started crying after an hour of interrogation. His alibi turned out to be solid, our next suspect Franklin Thomas aka Franklin Jefferson."

"He also has an alias."

"Well kind of, sort of, he had a previous record, dating some years back....

Brown took his fork, swirled it around some spaghetti and stuffed it into his mouth. Torres watched him; she took her fork and knife, cut into the chicken and waited for Brown to finish talking.

"...he had a domestic dispute with an ex girlfriend and it turned ugly. At the time, his parents thought it would be better to change his name."

"What led you two to believe he was a possible suspect?"

"His fingerprints were on Pamela Washington's dresser drawer. There was no indication he knew the first victim, but Homicide investigates all leads."

"So what happened with that?"

"Turns out he wasn't who we were looking for either. Whoever did these murders has to have a severe mental problem. Both those guys don't have what it takes to commit crimes of that nature."

"These days you never know who is capable of what."

"True, but not those guys... Franklin Jefferson maybe wanted to get in Pamela's pants or not. Boyd was a low-level drug dealer. Actually they both cried. No, not them- we're sure of it."

"What's next?"

"We keep looking until we find something solid."

Torres looked at Brown as he sighed, her eyes were focused.

"Anything wrong?"

"No, I'm just thinking about my mother. She was a very religious person. Oh, she went on and on about the Virgin Mary, Jesus, she drove me crazy. Church almost every Sunday."

"Real strict household."

"Something like that."

"I too have had my share of church, my mother would make me and my brother go faithfully. Do you still go to church?"

"I do when my mother asks me."

"Maybe I'll tag along one day, if you don't mind."

"No, I wouldn't mind, and my mom would love you. She'll say, 'Son, finally you brought a woman home I like'."

"So, Detective, where are we going with this?"

Brown understood and heard the question, but he never once really felt for a woman like he felt for Torres, not to mention, he just recently met her, but there was something about her he liked. He finished eating so he could answer her question. "Umm…how do I answer that question?"

"Just answer it." Brown used a napkin to wipe his mouth.

"We've been dating each other for a few days now, and I'm interested in you. I've had a few dates but no real relationships, so I was wondering how you feel about me. Are you the next level type of woman?"

The room became quiet all of a sudden; Brown thought everybody became quiet because they wanted to hear her respond. It was just his mind playing tricks on him. Brown never asked if anyone was interested in him, he was always asked that question and his answer was always-let's just be friends, let's take it slow. Torres smiled. "I like you," Torres wiped her mouth with her napkin. "I think there's a possibility that we can…"

Their conversation was interrupted- Brown's phone started ringing. It was the station calling. He answered the call, and after the brief conversation he stood up, waving to grab the attention of the waiter. He pulled two one-hundred dollars bills from his pocket and threw them on the table-that should cover the meal. He reached for Torres' hand to help her up out of her seat. Torres grabbed her napkin and wiped her mouth clean. "Maxwell, is everything ok?"

"We have to go, our friend struck again."

"Are you sure it's him?"

"I'm sure. The MO, unfortunately, is the same."

Not long after that was said Torres' phone rang, it was her office's overnight answering service giving her the news to report to a location. Without any doubt she knew it was the same location Brown received to report to. Handing the stub and a twenty to the valet, Brown got into the Jag, the valet holding the door open for Torres; she said "Thank you," and the Jaguar sped off, tires screeching.

Chapter 20

—

MEJAH BOOKSTORE, TRI-STATE MALL, CLAYMONT DELAWARE

The book signing of King's Palace kept Tamera busy; she was all over the spacious store, taking pictures and signing books. The sound of the cash register ringing as people bought her book was constant. Tamera was also making connections. She was introduced to some very important people in the publishing industry by the store's owner, whom everybody called Ms. M.

When Tamera's first book was published, she had been so excited; it'd made her feel like she had accomplished something. After finishing college and meeting Jones she'd felt complete, but knew there had to be more. So, she started to write again. It was something she'd always loved to do, but had never thought it would become a full-time job. But it had, and she loved every bit of it.

Jones stood off to the side, drinking a can of root beer and watching Tamera mingle. She had been doing this for four years now and was perfectly at ease. He focused his attention on a piece of artwork displayed on the wall that read, "Education before incarceration." He liked the store; the whole concept was about empowering one's self.

He glanced back at the crowd and saw Tamera coming toward him. To him, it was as if she was in slow motion. He took in every detail of her black dress and black heels, the dress showing off every curve on her body. She knew what to wear and worked the room with perfection: she was the whole package.

"So, how you doing over here, Jordan Jones?"

"I'm good. I see everything is going well tonight."

"Yeah, I'm surprised I'm liked in Delaware. Who would have thought?"

Putting his root beer on the nearest bookshelf he pulled her close to him, playing with her long, smooth ponytail. "You have to give yourself more credit than that. You wrote a good book and now, it's paying off."

Tamera gave him a quick kiss on the lips. "I guess you're right. Thanks to Ms. M., selling in this state was easy."

"Seems like a nice lady."

"Look at you, always in detective mode."

"Can't shake it sometimes...I'm sorry."

"No need to be sorry. My boyfriend is a detective. I can live with that." She kissed him again on the lips.

"You know, we do a lot of kissing."

"You're a good kisser. I could kiss you forever. You've been a little distant, though, lately. You're not cheating on me, are you?"

"Who, me? No way, José...we're in this together, forever."

Jones gave Tamera a big smile, they heard her name being called, turned around, and saw Ms. M. motioning her over.

"Duty calls. You ok?"

"Yeah, go ahead, baby, do your thing."

Chapter 21

—

TWO MORE BODIES

A few hours later, the drive back to New York was quiet, and the ride was smooth. Wrapped in a blanket, Tamera slept in the passenger seat while Jones drove, listening to the radio. He was bobbing his head up and down to Kanye West's "Can't Tell Me Nothing" when his phone rang.

"Jones, it's me, Brown."

He knew this couldn't be good and must have something to do with the case. "What's going on, Brown?"

"Bad news: another killing, only this time, there are two bodies."

"Brooklyn?"

"Yeah."

"I'm on the New Jersey Turnpike, exit twelve. I'm going to drop Tamera off, and I should be there within an hour and a half."

"I just got the call myself not too long ago. I'll see you there."

Jones put on the strobe and LED lights he had installed in his Tahoe some time ago and gunned it to over ninety miles per hour. The shock absorbers on the truck were so good Tamera didn't even move and stayed sound asleep until he dropped her off at home.

When he reached the location, Brown was already there, talking to Torres as they leaned against one of the police cars. Looking at the way they were dressed indicated something but Jones didn't ask, he just got out of the Tahoe and joined them.

"Brown, Torres."

Brown said, "Fifth floor, looks like our guy."

Following Brown and Torres up the stairs Jordan said,

"I see you're up late, Torres."

"I was having dinner when I got the call from my service. Brown informed me of the details."

"As soon as we catch this guy, you'll go back to the regular. But until then, we need to keep this quiet. Being that you were the first medical examiner on the scene, we need to keep you on call."

"I understand. Duty calls. This is what I signed up for, and I do love my job."

Jones said, "What do we have?"

Brown said, "A fourth floor tenant complained about water soaking through her bathroom ceiling. She knew the victim from seeing her around, so she went upstairs and knocked on the door. When she didn't get an answer, she phoned the on-call maintenance man. He came out to fix the problem, saw this, and called 911."

The first thing Jones noticed when they walked into the apartment was the huge water stain on the front door, the beginning of a trail throughout the apartment. They went deeper into the apartment and he saw the woman...same as the others.

Brown said, "Leslie Tomkins, age twenty-seven."

He walked towards the body, and in his mind it was confirmed. His killer had done this, the one he was looking for, the man he wanted to kill or not. Maybe he wanted to just catch him and do what he'd done to his victims over and over again until he screamed for mercy-until he begged Jones to kill him.

Torres said, "She was killed around eleven-thirty or midnight last night, same as the others. I've determined the same weapon used to mutilate the others was the same weapon used on the victim."

Jones turned and walked into the kitchen and saw the next victim on the floor bleeding from the head and neck. He noticed the broken pieces of a champagne bottle on the floor, its dried-up contents surrounding it.

Brown said, "Michael Weeks, Jr. His wallet was in his back pocket. It looks like there was a struggle. Maybe he walked in, saw what was going on, and tried to stop it, but the killer got the best of him."

Jones said, "This bottle on the floor-looks to me he was caught by surprise and stabbed in the back. Then the killer slammed the knife into his head then he stabbed him in the neck, killing him instantly. What's your professional point of view, Torres?"

"Whether he was caught by surprise, I don't know, my professional opinion is he came down on his head first with the blade." Torres walked over and pointed to the indentations on the body's head. "You see here and here. The blade wasn't strong enough to penetrate the skull so he found a more vulnerable spot and stabbed him in the neck once, then came down on his back once, killing him. I estimate the time of death to be some time yesterday. I'll confirm my findings when I get the bodies autopsied. The good news is I have something this time that will definitely help you, detectives."

Jones said, "What's that?"

Brown said, "He had this underneath his fingernail." Brown held up a small plastic bag. Inside was a strand of hair.

"The male victim grabbed at his killer, maybe trying to hold on in some kind of defensive position, and pulled this tiny piece of evidence."

Jones said, "So there was a struggle, and they say dead people can't talk."

Chapter 22

WORKSHOP/SOMEWHERE IN NEW YORK CITY

Clad in nothing but his skin, the killer awoke screaming but there was no sound, grabbing at his throat. Grabbing at his head, the pain he endured for some time has come to once again bring the monster out of him. Then the memory of his kills flooded his mind-

Picking up his van keys, and loading his project he left his residence. The van pulled out of the driveway and headed south, it was cold outside and his jacket provided just enough material he needed to stay warm and move with flexibility. Holding a piece of paper in his hand, eyes focused on its contents. His attention on the sheet of paper caused him to make a sharp right turn, which caused the wood in the back of van to slide to the left. He almost went in the wrong direction, his mind now focused on his destination and his eyes wavering back and forth to the road and navigation system to make sure he stayed on track, minutes later he was at his destination, and he stopped abruptly when he saw his next victim.

He'd slammed down on the brakes immediately, and the driver behind had done the same a split second later to avoid running into the back of the van. The driver of the car had swerved around him, honking and yelling. He gave the killer the finger and yelled, "Asshole," as he sped by.

The killer had looked at the car passing him and resisted the urge to chase the driver down, snatch him out of the car, and break his neck. Instead, he remained calm and focused on his prey. He watched the woman as she went into Pathmark. He pulled into the parking lot and continued to follow her into the store. Once inside, he rubbed his hands together, cupped them, and then blew his hot breath into them. They'd been so cold.

He watched her as she took off her hat. Pretty, he thought. She'd taken off her jacket, grabbed a cart, put her pocketbook into it, and started shopping. She moved about the store, oblivious to the fact she was being watched. She'd gone into the beverage aisle and had been picky, trying to find the right bottle of wine. As she picked up ingredients for side dishes, he'd focused on her shape. She'd worn a tight, black, knitted sweater that made her breasts look full, and the cool temperature made her nipples erect. The sweater had been stuffed into tight blue jeans that emphasized her round buttocks as she walked.

Once she had finished shopping, she made her way to the cashier, paid for her items, and headed to a late model Audi A3. She loaded her groceries, got into her car, and drove off. He hurried into his van and followed her to a *building in the Park Slope area of downtown Brooklyn. He parked the van near the corner, got out, and watched her as she took her groceries from the car and into the building. She returned back to her car, opened up the backseat door, and was reaching for her briefcase when her cell phone rang. She knew who it was and had been waiting for the call, face glowing, she paced herself, she wanted to act surprised.*

Preoccupied by her call, the killer slipped past the woman unnoticed, and made his way quickly to her apartment building.

"Hi, Michael."

"Hey, Leslie, I'm back in town, and thought I'd come over and see you."

"How was your trip?"

"It was good, but it would have been better if you were there with me."

"Now, we've been through that, Michael. I'm on my way into my building – been working late all week. But I'll be ready in about twenty minutes. I'll see you then."

"Ok, I'm on my way." The killer quickly made his way to her second floor apartment and used slim metal tools to gain entrance inside.

She walked into the lobby of the building, got her mail, and headed up to her second floor apartment. Once inside, she put her briefcase, mail, and pocketbook on the kitchen counter. She went to the refrigerator, took out the chicken already in a roasting pan, put it in the oven, and proceeded to her bedroom. She went into the bathroom, turned on the water in her bathtub, and undressed. She stood in front of the mirror to put up her hair.

There was movement in the apartment, but she didn't hear anything because the killer moved like a snake in grass stalking his prey in the night. He stood out of her line of vision, watching her naked body and becoming aroused. He thought to himself, "She would make a nice sacrifice". She put a robe on and went to get her mail, and she saw something out of the corner of her eye. She stopped in her tracks and saw a huge cross up against her living room wall. While she was thinking that it was some kind of weird joke, she was grabbed from behind. She struggled with her attacker, kicking her legs wildly, but the man was too strong. She could smell the chloroform and feel the pressure from the strong hand pushing down on her nose. She also felt the liquid entering her nostrils every time she took a breath. Then, she felt herself slowly fading away, and there was blackness. He picked her up and started strapping her to the cross when he heard the door opening. He quickly hid in a corner of the living room and left her right arm dangling. He pulled out his knife and waited.

"It's me, baby. Sorry, I could've gotten here sooner, but I stopped to pick up some bubbly."

Michael heard the bathwater running, so he went into the kitchen and started rummaging through the drawers, a bottle of champagne in one hand. The knife came down into his back, hard, and Michael let out a gasp as the knife was snatched out. The pain was unbearable; he turned around, falling up against the counter. The champagne fell on its side and rolled off the counter, crashing onto the floor. Michael grasped at the killer's head with one hand and grabbed him by his shirt with the other, but he was too weak from the hit in the back to fight back. He was losing blood rapidly. The blood soaking his shirt was making its way down to his jeans. The killer grabbed Michael by the throat. Michael grabbed the killer's wrist with both hands to free himself, but the killer's grip was locked, crushing his throat. The killer was too strong...

The killer saw the fear in Michael's eyes. The fear made it easier for him. He brought the twelve-inch blade down into Michael's head twice but it wouldn't penetrate his skull so he stabbed him in the neck. He pushed it and pushed it until the blade couldn't be seen anymore and quickly pulled it out. The ridges on the blade had meat on them when he pulled it out. Then, he watched as Michael fell to the floor. Blood gushed out of Michael's neck, as he lay on the floor with eyes wide open.

The killer looked at the lifeless body, and images started to flash in his mind. He held his hands up and grabbed his head, trying to shake the vision from appearing. But he couldn't...the vision became clearer, and he found himself remembering his first murder when he was twenty-one. His father had come home to find his son covered in blood and naked, on his knees in the dining room with a crazed expression on his face. He clutched a kitchen knife in his right hand, blood dripping from it.

"Boy, what happened here? Do you hear me? What happened?"

"God told me to do it?"

His father had knelt down and put his hands on his son's shoulders. He looked past his son and saw his wife's mutilated body on the kitchen room floor. His parents had always known there was something wrong with him, but never imagined he would become a murderer and spend years in mental institutions with constant counseling.

The killer came out from his brief vision, stepped over Michael's body, and headed for Leslie. She was regaining consciousness and through her blurred vision saw him coming as he stood in front of her.

"Do you know that Jesus was crucified for our sins, and we take what happened to him for granted?"

That brought on a migraine headache that was taking its toll. Standing, grabbing his Bible, he dropped it. Still no sound, mouth wide, gazing into nothingness, lifting his arms, standing still, strips of skin on his back ripped opened and blood came from nowhere around his head. Blood formed around his wrists, feet bleeding, and then falling to his knees. The awful visions, the unbearable pain, instantly went away. Quickly getting dressed, he made his way to his work area.

The sound of sand paper was soothing to the ear, that and his breathing was the only thing that could be heard in the quiet room cluttered with saws, drills, hammers every tool he needed was in this little room. This is where he felt most comfortable. The killer stood over an old wooden table. He moved his hand up and down, sanding away, at times taking a moment to feel the smooth edges of his project or stopping to look at a picture of Jesus Christ on the wall above his work area.

He continued on a project he had been working on for some time-he called it an epiphany- after several attempts of carving a piece of wood to his satisfaction, he finally did it. He carefully carved out a small piece of wood into a smooth handle; he held it as if it gave him power beyond anyone's recognition but his own.

The steel had to be right; putting on heavy duty gloves and cutting goggles he grabbed the oxygen acetylene torch and started to shape a piece of steel, he was being led by a godly force or so he thought. The sparks shot up in the air and exploded on the plastic goggles, it didn't disturb him though, he just continued cutting and cutting, shaping the steel to what looked like a sword when he finished.

—

FINALLY A LEAD/TWO DAYS LATER/FRIDAY

Jones got a call from Larry, who said the knives from Mr. Jefferson's apartment weren't a match to the mutilation of any of the bodies. Two days had passed since the third and fourth bodies had been found, and the investigation in the victims' lives left Jones and Brown with the same thing: nothing. Even the DNA from the strand of hair left no answers because it didn't match anybody in the database. But it was a piece of evidence that they both hoped would play its part, sooner or later. Both detectives felt they had covered every angle that would connect the victims. They looked into locksmiths, gardeners, auto shops, gyms, and professions: everything. And yet, they felt they were still at the beginning.

Jones sat at his desk, yawning, waiting for Brown to come in. As usual, he was late. His tardiness used to bother him, but now he was accustomed to it because Brown always brought coffee for the both of them, and it always hit the spot.

"Sorry I'm late, Jones…here, brought you a cup."

"No problem, Brown. Thanks."

Then the phone rang. "Detective Jordan Jones speaking. How can I help you?"

"Jones, I have some hits for you. I found seven places that carry dogwood. I just emailed the list to you."

"Great. Thanks, Larry."

Chapter 24

—

THE PAIN I ENDURE/LOCATION UNKNOWN

The horse bucked as the 24-inch whip hit its backside making the other horses move wildly about, breaking formation.

Five Roman soldiers on black stallions, a well-armored hit squad came into the village. Four of them descended then drew their swords. The leader, still mounted, barked an order and watched as the four took to swinging their weapons, killing men, women and children on sight.

The screaming was the worst, he felt as if his eardrums were going to explode. He watched in horror as people were getting their throats cut, and blood splattered everywhere. People were on their knees begging for their lives, praying for mercy, praying for Jesus to help them.

He knew this was a dream, a dream or a vision that he'd been having since he was thirteen but as the years went by the pain became greater, uncontrollable and at twenty-one he couldn't take the pain any longer. It didn't matter, whatever it was, he couldn't wake up, no matter how hard he tried. Homes in the village were now all engulfed in flames, the same scenario nothing changes. Then they see him, the leader speaks "You there, what's your name boy?" He can talk, but for some reason he can't, so he says nothing and every time it angers the one in charge.

The leader dismounts, he's the meanest of the bunch, a loyal pawn for the Roman Empire. The sun hits his armor and shines in his eyes blinding him for a second, giving one of the four the opportunity to get behind him, and he knocks him to his knees.

It was a dream, a nightmare, a vision that appeared whether he was sleeping or awake, awake in the sense he didn't know what was happening to him, like a seizure that has to take its course.

The leader's sword was at the tip of his chin; he put it under his chin and with it, the Roman soldier lifted his chin, bringing his head up so that he could be eye level with him. The tip of the sword was so sharp it pierced his skin; minuscule sized drops of blood hit the dirt. He looked into the soldier's eyes, there were no eyes, there was nothing, darkness, soulless, "I asked you who are you?" Again he struggled to speak but nothing. The solider stared at him, dark smoke coming out his eyes twirling upwards.

His mouth moved, but he didn't have control of it or control of what he was saying. "I'm Jesus," as much as he didn't want to say it, it was said. He wanted to tell them that this isn't real; I'm not Jesus. But like always, he said it and like always, the torture came afterwards. "What treachery is this?" the solider yelled. "Jesus, he was nailed to a cross. I saw him die, you want to be Jesus then suffer the fate he did." He knew what was coming next, after having this dream/vision for years, the torture, the pain, and the cries of the people. The dead bodies left after the violent wave of pure savagery. He was done. Not anymore. Why should he suffer the pain, why, why, why……

He didn't give in, he fought like he always did, but it was no use. The other three soldiers went to the aid of their comrade and wrestled him to the ground. The four soldiers held him down as the leader pulled his whip from its casing connected to the saddle, his was different, the thin black strips of leather were longer and each end had five sharp metal pieces on the tip of them.

Shaking uncontrollably he stood up in the room and extended his arms, it was happening again, the dream becoming more realistic. "Wake up," he shouted, "not again!" Why, he asked himself, didn't he sacrifice enough? Did more blood have to be spilled?

He braced himself; he knew what was coming next. The four men held onto his arms and then it happened. The hand gripped the handle, swinging his arm forward the leather straps came down, the metal pieces ripped into his body, five slashes, ten slashes, fifthteen slashes, blood splatter showered the soldiers bodies.

The Roman came down again, and again, and again. He screamed- his eyes bloodshot red, baring white teeth. It was horrible; his flesh slit open, meat hanging, saturated blood dripped from the metal pieces.

Then the crown of meshed thorns, slammed onto his head, more blood. Head hanging, on all fours in excruciating pain the soldiers picked him up and held him up against a wooden cross that just appeared out of nowhere.

Then he suddenly found himself unable to move; simultaneously the soldiers jammed three long wide nails into him. One through his feet, the other two through his hands, he screamed, on the verge of passing out he heard the voice again like clockwork, "Kill for me." Then he awoke.

Naked he stood vertical, both arms horizontal, his body still suffering the agony, trembling, he fell to the floor, gasping for air, grabbing his throat. It took a little while before the pain subsided, but it didn't go away completely. He knew what he had to do; he had already located his next victim. Been watching her for a few days trying to decide when the time was right to do it. Now was the time.

Chapter 25

—

My 21ˢᵀ Birthday

The van pulled onto the street, it was quiet, and today was much colder than yesterday he thought. The night always brought the cold with it, and it had a way of seeping through your clothes, and wrapping itself around your body.

He thought of his mother while he sat welcoming the heat, deciding if one more should be sacrificed. He didn't tell anybody about the dream, the vision, for fear he would be looked at as a freak by his mother and father, friends and family, so he kept it to himself.

Blasphemy would have been a word his father would have used and he would've been an outcast from that point on. It turned out he ended up that way anyway. He had just come out of a mentally horrific episode and heard his mother calling him. The pain hadn't diminished but he held it together and made his way into the dining room where she been preparing the table for dinner. She smiled when he finally came down, "What were you doing up there?"

"Nothing, just messing around that's all."

"It'll be your 21st birthday tomorrow- any thoughts on what you want?"

"I haven't really thought about it, to tell you the truth"

"Maybe a new car?" She smiled showing her white teeth, walking around the table setting the plates in their spots for his father and for him.

"That'll be nice." His body shivering, he paused just to catch himself from falling. "Are you ok?" she asked.

"Think I'm coming down with a cold or something." She came over to him and put her hand on his head, he wasn't warm, he was cold as ice. "Come into the kitchen and let me make you a cup of hot chocolate. You're freezing." They entered the kitchen, he took a seat on one of the stools next to the kitchen countertop and was forcing himself not to shake, the pain just wouldn't go away.

This time he felt different.

His mother on her tippy toes was grabbing at a coffee cup, holding onto one of the shelves for support. The shelf gave way, glasses and plates came tumbling down, crashing onto the floor, one plate smashed onto her right hand slashing it between the thumb and forefinger, blood swooshed out and splattered on the floor, over her clothes. He ran over to help her and grabbed her hand, there was so much blood that blood rested on his hand and the pain he felt was slowly fading away.

Blood was blood the cure, was blood what he needed to wipe his pain away? He held onto her hand, his grip tightening. She looked at him. "I'm ok honey, grab a napkin off the table there." He didn't respond he took his hand and patted the gash on her hand and blood was on the tip of his fingers. He raised his hand, looked at it and put it on his face. She was pulling her hand away but his grip on it was tighter. "You're scaring me, let me go." Refreshing, this was it the cure for his pain. The next thing he knew he had a 12-inch knife in his hand. She was screaming now but he didn't hear her.

The knife slit her throat first, she grabbed at her throat with her left hand and stumbled into the kitchen counter top, he wanted to stop but in his trance-like state he couldn't, he continued to mutilate her. The last thing he remembered was when his father came home and being driven away in a police car.

His father had come home to find his son covered in blood and naked, on his knees in the dining room with a crazed expression on his face. He'd clutched a kitchen knife in his right hand, blood dripping from it.

"Boy, what happened here? Do you hear me? What happened?"

"God told me to do it?"

His father had knelt down and put his hands on his son's shoulders. He'd looked past his son and had seen his wife's mutilated body on the kitchen room floor.

Focusing now on his next victim, he took a look at the words etched on a small piece of metal leading into the supposed gated community.

Park Slope Town Houses.

Chapter 26

DENVER, COLORADO

Monday morning after checking out six out of seven locations in three days, the last led the detectives to book the
earliest flight available to the Denver International Airport.
During the four-hour flight, Brown sat by the window in one
of the last rows, listening to his iPod, while Jones sat next to
him, alternating between reading Patricia Cornwell's *Scar-
petta* and making notes on the case.

As soon as they landed and stopped at the gate, Brown
stood up and grabbed their bags from the overhead bin. He
handed Jones his, stepped in front of an old lady and a little
boy, and made his way off the plane. Then Jones stood up,
waited for three people to pass him by, and was the last one
off. When he finally reached the baggage claim area, he saw
Brown talking to a police officer. He was carrying a white
cardboard sign with their names on it. He walked up to them,
and the officer extended his hand and said, "Officer Hill, at
your service."

"You new to the force?"

"Just started about six months ago. How you'd guess?"

Brown said, "My partner has a knack for picking out rookies."

Officer Hill was young and clean cut: early twenties, white male, dark black hair, and a muscular, fit build. His uniform fit him perfectly. He looked more like a state trooper than a city police officer.

"I'm Detective Jones, and I see you already met my partner."

"Yes, sir, I have."

"Have you been briefed on the situation?"

"I have…I was told to escort you two detectives wherever you want to go."

"Good. There's no time to waste. We need to get to this location ASAP. We have a few questions to ask the owners."

Officer Hill took the sheet of paper Jones pulled out of his pocket and read it out loud.

"Orchard City, Smalls Incorporated, 11130 Antelope Road. That's the Smalls' place. It's just off Route 65 – we'll be there in a jiffy."

They left the terminal and headed for a police-issue Ford Bronco. It was cold outside and they were all glad to get into the vehicle. Once inside, Officer Hill got on the radio.

"This is Hill. I'm taking our guests over to Orchard City."

"That's a ten-four," the dispatcher said.

Jones asked, "You know the place?"

"You bet. Everybody knows the place. Most of the people in the area get firewood and Christmas trees from the old man."

"So you know him well?"

"Well enough…why do you ask? Is he in any trouble?"

"Don't know yet. We'll have to talk to him and see."

"He's an old man. I doubt if he'll give anybody any trouble…now, his son, that's another matter."

"Why do you say that?"

"The boy, he's some sort of religious freak, you know."

"Are the Smalls churchgoing people?"

"The old man was a preacher some years ago. He had a small congregation."

"What about the son now?"

"He was always a problem kid, smart, though, real smart. I was a junior and he was a senior. But I heard the weird stuff he would do to be part of the in crowd, you know. So it wasn't a surprise when he killed his mother five years ago – did a real butcher job on her, too. He was sent away to the crazy house."

"Do you know what institution he was sent to?"

"White Stead Mental Facility, way up in the mountains." This had to be the man the detectives were looking for, it had to be. Jones had found the killer or so he hoped. "He's not there anymore though."

"Where is he?"

Chapter 27

—

THREE WEEKS AGO

Located in the mountains of San Juan, Colorado, White Stead Mental Facility is home to the state's most dangerous mental patients. Attendant Rick Waters' partner had retired and left him to train and get to know another partner. Rick had kept himself in shape to handle any problems that might occur. At forty-six years of age, five feet tall, and two hundred pounds, his physical frame alone still commanded respect.

"Mr. Waters"

Putting on his work shirt with his back to the door, Rick was caught off guard. He turned around. "I'm Waters. Are you the new guy? Steven?"

Buttoning his shirt Rick stood sizing up his new partner.

"Yes, that's me. I didn't mean to startle you. How are you?" Steven said as he reached out to shake Rick's hand.

"I'm ok. Call me Rick," he said as he took a ring of about fifty keys out of his pocket and locked the locker room door. He then shook Steven's hand, took a look at his watch. "You're right on time. Let's get started. Here's your time card. Go ahead and punch in. The time clock is right over there. I'll fill you in on the routine and rules while we walk."

"Ok."

The two walked and Rick explained in detail a list of rules and regulations. Then the mention of food came up.

"Any good places to eat around here?"

"Not much, but there's a pizza place not too far from here. I go there from time to time, not bad."

"I hear your old partner retired, twenty-five years in the place. I wonder if I'll last that long."

Stopping at the kitchen.

"The old man taught me everything I know, and I've survived for five years. So you'll last – just remember, never deviate from the rules, and you'll be all right. Take these, your set of keys. Let's get to work. It's breakfast time, and if you're late, them nut jobs give you problems all day.

Ok, there's four parts to this institution. North, East, South and West. Right now we're heading to the west wing, also known as level three. That's where the most dangerous patients are housed. I know them boys are hungry right about now, so grab that wheel cart, and let's go. Never go into the west wing alone. Always remember that.

There are four patients in this section. Mr. Witherspoon, he believes all children are demons, and it's his job to kill them all. Mr. Davis, he killed his whole family and started killing people at random. He went to prison, killed two guards and one inmate. He thinks that every human is infected with some sort of disease and he must get rid of them. Mr. Ross, he scratches himself until he bleeds. They have him on medication most of the time. Why he does it, I don't know. You see that lotion on that shelf over there? Uses it all...one whole bottle a day."

"What's in it?"

"Don't know, but whatever it is, it stops him from scratching. This room here is Travis Smalls, a real psycho. Looks like one, too. Grab that tray. I heard down in the kitchen he killed his mother or sister, something like that, for his sins or hers. I don't know for sure, and I don't want to know, but I know he's some sort of a religious freak."

Rick was looking for the key to open the door, Steven stood holding the tray of food. He took a look through the square window reinforced with steel wire and saw Travis sitting in a chair with his back facing the door. Rick opened the door, and Steven walked in. The room was spotless; every room in all of the buildings was painted white, but there was something different about this one. The bed looked as if Travis didn't even sleep in it, and everything was in perfect order. The only thing that stood out was his Bible.

Rick said, "Travis, what's up, buddy?"

Travis was sitting motionless. There was complete silence for a second, then, "Ah, Rick, I was beginning to think you'd forgotten about me this morning. Who's your friend?"

Keeping one hand on the club hanging from his belt, Rick motioned to Steven with his other hand to put the tray of food on the table. Steven did so, and then took a step back.

"This is Steven. He's going to be my new partner."

"Well, let's take a look at him."

Travis stood up and turned around, Steven didn't know what to say or think. The man looked like Charles Manson. His face was mostly covered with a full beard that was unkempt, and he had a head full of hair. He looked to be about six feet tall and two hundred and ten, maybe fifteen, pounds. Steven didn't say it out loud, but to him, this guy looked like he needed to be in a straitjacket. Steven could see him breaking someone's neck quickly. Steven was a comic book reader, and to him, Travis looked like a super villain. The pants he wore were tight enough to show that his thighs were all muscle. The v-necked shirt collar showed his huge neck and shoulders, and the short sleeves revealed thick forearms and biceps. His chest stuck out like a lion's, as if he was king of the jungle, but he spoke peacefully and elegantly.

"How are you, Steven?" Travis said as he extended his hand with a big smile on his face. Steven went to shake it, but Rick stopped him in his tracks by putting his club on Steven's hand and lowering it.

"Travis, now you know there's no physical contact."

Steven pushed the club away and said, "Rick, calm down, I got this. What's up, man? I'm the new man on the block. You got to excuse the old timer," Steven said as he shook Travis' hand. He stood to the side of Rick and said, "I see you're into your Bible."

"Why, yes, I read the Bible to keep my sanity. Are you a religious man, Steven?"

"No, not really."

Rick interrupted the conversation. "Ok, that's enough. Travis, enjoy your breakfast. Steven, let's go. We have work to do."

Rick closed the door and double-checked it to make sure it was locked. Steven took a look through the window and saw Travis sitting down like he was when they first came to the door.

"Steven, grab the cart, and let's move on. I want you to listen to me very carefully: that man and all the men in this section are here for a purpose, remember that. Your job during breakfast, lunch, and dinner is to give them their trays and move on. When they are to be transferred around the facility you are to get me…never go alone. No physical contact at all. Remember that. Also remember, procedure on all Doctor Visits with patients. You enter first, walk behind the patient and apply the arm restraints; you'll see them hanging from every chair in all the patients rooms. These sessions the doctors have with these nuts are confidential. We can't stay in the room with them; we maintain a constant visual by looking through the glass mirror on the doors every five minutes."

"I understand."

A few hours later.

After a morning of learning the routine from Rick, Steven paused at the large windows that surrounded the building, where he could hear the wind outside blowing hard against them. The windows had to be forty feet high and forty feet wide. Steven looked out the window at the snow surrounding the area where he stood. The snow was so high that it covered at least two feet of the window. He took in the huge mountains and watched the wind blow snow off tall trees.

Suddenly, a commotion broke out further down the hall. "Let's go." Rick yelled. Rick and Steven took off running in that direction and brought down a patient who was giving a doctor a hard time.

"Dr. O'Donnell, are you ok?"

"I'm ok. Rick, you two hold him down while I get this needle ready."

Steven was able to get the patient in a headlock while Rick held the man's arms behind him.

"This will just take a second…there, I got it. Ok, hold his arms tight."

Dr. O'Donnell held the needle up to her eyes to make sure the dosage was correct. She squeezed out some of the liquid from the needle and then stuck it in the arm of the patient. The patient struggled for several minutes more and then slowly fell into an unconscious state. His body fell limp, and then Rick and Steven carried him into his room and strapped him to his bed.

"I want to thank you two for coming to my rescue. He's never acted like that before."

"Don't worry about it, Dr. O'Donnell, just glad to be of some help. I keep telling you doctors to not go to these rooms alone because anything can happen," Rick said as he locked the patient's door and double-checked it to make sure it was secure.

"I know you have on many occasions, Rick. I should have called someone to meet me here, but I thought I was making progress with the patient. He's level one…my recommendation will be to put him into level two."

"Even with the level ones, I believe you doctors should still have escorts. Oh, by the way, this is Steven. He's my new partner."

Steven shook the doctor's hand and made a face as he said, "Hi, I'm Steven, the new guy."

Dr. O'Donnell gave a little laugh and responded, "Hello, I'm Dr. O'Donnell. I'm the resident psychiatrist."

"This is his training day. Tomorrow, though, it'll be official."

Steven said, "Hope I live up to the task."

"I'm sure you'll do just fine, young man," Dr. O'Donnell said as she bent down to pick up her clipboard and paperwork.

Rick said, "So who's up for an out today, doc? Steven, Doc O'Donnell counsels and determines if it's time for a patient to be released."

"Travis is. Gentlemen, once again, I want to thank you two for the help, and Steven, I'll see you around."

They both watched her walk away and looked at each other. Rick said, "Boy, don't even think about it."

Shrugging his shoulders, Steven said, "What, I didn't see a ring or nothing, and she's smoking hot."

"Come on...grab the cart and let's go to lunch. Did you bring lunch or are you going out?"

"I'm gonna go out."

"Be back by one o'clock, and come straight down to the maintenance room. I'll be in there."

"Ok, see you then."

At one o' clock, Steven had just walked into the building and was on his way to meet up with Rick when he was stopped by Dr. O'Donnell.

"Steven, Steven, I'm glad I caught you. Can you escort me to Travis' room? It's time for his one o'clock session."

"Guess I can do that. Let me just radio Rick to let him know."

"Ok."

Steven pulled out his radio and pressed on the black button on the side.

"Rick, come in."

"Go."

"Dr. O'Donnell wants me to escort her to the west wing for her one o'clock session with Travis Smalls."

"Ok, I'll meet you two there. Wait for me at the west entrance. I'm busy in the east wing with the cook preparing trays for dinner. I'll be there in about twenty minutes."

"Ten-four. Will do, boss."

After radioing Rick, Steven and Dr. O'Donnell headed for the west wing. The smell of disinfectant in the halls made them cover their noses as they watched two maintenance men mop the floors.

"They sure keep this place clean as a whistle."

Dr. O'Donnell's long black hair swung to her right as she looked at Steven and said, "They do. So, how do like the job so far?"

"Right now, I really don't have any complaints."

"Think you'll be here in twenty-five years?"

"There's a good possibility I will. How long have you been working here?"

"I've been here five years now. It's been good. I've been building my experience to maybe open my own private practice."

"I could see that happening for you. Maybe I'll be working for you one day."

"Maybe. You never know."

"Ok, let me open the door."

"Shouldn't we wait for Rick?"

"He'll be here. Something must have held him up. Don't worry, I got this, doctor."

Steven opened the door and found Travis sitting in his chair, facing the door this time. The Doctor walked in as Steven stood in the doorway. When the Doctor sat, following procedure Steven walked behind Travis and strapped his wrists to the chair. Steven then left the room but stood on the opposite side of the door and watched them through the square window.

"Travis, how are you today?"

"I'm doing fine, Doctor, how are you?"

"I'm doing well. Next month will be five years since you came here, Travis," the Doctor said.

"Yes, it will."

Pushing her glasses up over the rim of her nose and opening a folder, the Doctor asked, "Is there anything you want to ask me before I make my decision on your status here at the facility?"

"No, but there is something I've been planning to do for two years now. Before, God told me I wasn't ready, but God says I am now."

Looking over pages inside the folder, Dr. O'Donnell took off her glasses, looked at Travis. "And what would that be, Travis?"

With lighting speed and unbelievable strength, Travis' right hand rose, breaking the armrest off the chair with the strap still attached to his wrist. He reached over the table and grabbed Dr. O'Donnell by her throat, crushing it. She grabbed his arm with both hands as she gasped for air. Her facial expression revealed fear and pain. As Travis stood up, he shook his left hand free and threw the table between the two of them. It hit the wall, alerting Steven, who had been daydreaming. Steven opened the door and rushed in to help Dr. O'Donnell. He pulled out his club and headed towards Travis. Travis threw Dr. O'Donnell against the wall, hitting her head and knocking her unconscious.

Then, he collided with Steven. The force of his body knocked Steven up against the door, dazing him. Travis looked at him, moving about trying to regain his composure. The club was a foot away; Travis picked it up and came down hard on Steven's head, killing him instantly. Travis took Steven's uniform off his body and put it on. He wanted to kill the doctor, too, but there wasn't time to do it properly. He rummaged through her pockets and took her keys. Time was of the essence; after being in the facility for five years, Travis had the routine down to a science.

He quickly picked up Steven and put him into the bed and covered the body with the bright white sheet. He picked up the doctor and placed her in the closet. The halls were empty, his plan worked like a charm, and he escaped the building without incident. Once outside, he walked into the parking lot, used Dr. O'Donnell's car remote to find her Nissan Pathfinder, got in, and drove away.

Chapter 28

THE SMALLS' RESIDENCE

Brown said, "So, he got away."

"Sure did. We've been looking for him ever since. Doctor O'Donnell put in the call about 2:30pm to alert authorities of his escape. Security officers, police officers including myself combed the grounds for him, and then we put out roadblocks covering all the main roads. It was snowing hard that night…kind of like Mother Nature helped him get away. He killed an attendant during the escape, bashed his head in with a stick or something. He's a brute this one, a real big mean son of a bitch. "

"We'll need to talk to the Doctor and read over the police report. And we'll need to get a photo of him ASAP."

"I'll do better than that. I have the wanted poster of him in the truck." Officer Hill reached into the glove compartment and pulled out two posters of Travis. "Here we go." He handed posters to Brown and Jones, and they looked them over. Jones pulled out his Blackberry, knowing it would come in handy one day. He took a picture of the poster and forwarded it to Larry with a text that read, "Notify Captain, possible suspect in killings: Travis Smalls. Have photos made but hold off on distribution until further notice."

The Bronco climbed up a hill, and they stopped in front of the driveway. There was a chain blocking the way up, so they all got out of the truck.

Brown said, "Looks like nobody's home."

Jones said, "Do you have anything to cut that chain?"

"Should have, give me a second. I think I have some cutters in the back."

Officer Hill went to the back of the Bronco, and Brown walked up beside Jones and said, "I think we found our man."

"An escaped patient from a mental facility. Go figure. I think all we have to do now is apprehend him."

Officer Hill came back with a big pair of chain cutters used on police raids. "This should work, fellas."

Officer Hill cut the chain with one snap, and they got back into the Bronco and drove up the long, slush-covered driveway. They stopped in front of the house. The house was European and well crafted. It had to be at least four thousand square feet. The Smalls had done well for themselves. There were maybe three or four acres of land covered with a blanket of snow. The church was to the right, and further down, the business stood on the left. They all could see the

Smalls name printed in black over the door. The house was in the middle.

Brown said, "Looks creepy, doesn't it?"

Jones said, "Yeah, it does."

Officer Hill and Brown stood by Jones, they all looked at the place. Officer Hill walked up to the door with Brown and Jones following. He knocked on it three times, but no one answered.

Jones pulled out his weapon and Officer Hill and Brown followed suit. Jones reached for his picking tools to open the door, but Officer Hill stopped him.

"Don't we need a warrant?"

Holding up his handgun, Detective Jones said, "This is my warrant. We'll split up. I'll take the house. Hill, take the church. Brown, you take the business. If you find anything, holler out."

Chapter 29

—

The house-The church-The Business

Detective Jones pulled out his tools, inserted one in the lock, and click, click, the door opened. He entered with his weapon in a two-handed grip in front of him. He didn't know what to expect, so he moved about the house cautiously.

Officer Hill walked up to the church and pushed open the door. He unclipped the leather strap that held his firearm in place and entered. The church was all white and appeared godly, but he had a creepy feeling about the place. There were eight rows of benches on both sides and eight windows, all with white and black crosses painted on them. He took additional steps into the church to investigate.

Detective Brown walked up to the one-story building and turned the doorknob. The door was locked, so he used his elbow to break one of its four, square windows. He stuck his hand in and was able to reach the knob and open the door making a creaking sound as it did. He took out his gun, held it down to his side, and went in. He came to double doors with a sign above them that read, "Woodshop."

Detective Jones continued into the house and entered the kitchen, where there was a marble island and a rack of pots and pans suspended over it. The island was littered with newspapers and envelopes. He stopped to pick up one of them, and it appeared to be junk mail. He walked over to the Subzero refrigerator made of stainless steel and could see a smudgy reflection of himself on the door. The double sink had a dirty plate in it and a half empty glass of something colorful. The dining room area was classy but needed house-keeping. Every piece of furniture was dusty. He used two fingers to wipe dust off a hanging lamp that was positioned directly in the center of the table. He didn't see anything out of the ordinary, so he went on.

Off the dining room area was a home office. He went inside and headed straight to the desk. He put his gun down and searched the drawers, hoping to find something impor-tant. He found receipts, credit cards, and an address book. Inside were business locations and phone numbers. He took the book and continued searching. Jones focused his atten-tion on a computer. The computer had to have something on it, but he knew this was not his expertise. He made a mental note of its location so it could be confiscated for evidence later. If there was anything on its drives, he was sure Larry would find it. Finding nothing else useful, he headed up-stairs. There were three bedrooms. Using his gun to nudge the doors open, he found nothing out of the ordinary there, either. Then he heard a noise.

Detective Brown hadn't realized the place was so spacious from the outside. There were tables with vice grips attached to them. Forklifts were parked against the wall, and the floor was covered with wood dust. As he got closer to the middle of the shop, he heard a rumbling noise.

Officer Hill walked to the far end of the church and looked at the life-size statue of Jesus lying on the floor. The paint on the wall in front of him was white, but a cross-shaped portion of the wall wasn't painted. He saw the cross, cracked into two pieces, lying by the podium. He didn't know what to make of it, but it looked as if the cross had been ripped off the wall. Then he heard a noise, so he turned to his right and saw a door. He pushed it open and saw nothing but darkness. There was an overwhelming odor coming from the dark. He took out his thirty-eight and his flashlight, saw stairs, and made his way down them.

Detective Jones was sure the noise came from the master bedroom. So with caution, he walked into the room and heard the noise again. He knelt down and looked under the bed – nothing. He went into the closet and saw nothing but clothes. Then, he heard it again.

Detective Brown focused his attention on the noise, trying to pinpoint its exact location. It took him to a staircase with seven steps going down. When he reached the bottom, he realized he was in a machine shop. The noise was clearer now, so he raised his gun and kept walking towards it.

Officer Hill was afraid. He wouldn't admit it to anybody else, but he couldn't lie to himself. His heart was racing, and he couldn't determine if he heard or felt his heart pounding. Six months on the force and he'd never come close to pulling his firearm, but today he'd actually felt it necessary. He came to the bottom of the steps, using the flashlight to canvass the room. He stood by the steps for a second just to get control of himself. His heart was racing and his hands were shaking. Count down from twenty to one, he thought, something he did to govern himself mentally and physically.

Detective Jones moved the clothes hanging in the closet. He looked up and saw a trap door. An attic, he thought. There was a ladder held up on a hook. He put his gun in his holster and released the hook and the ladder slowly came down. It came down in two seconds but it felt like it took forever. With caution he went up the ladder and pushed on the trap door. It wouldn't budge at first, but after a few pushes it moved. He went up into the attic and could've sworn somebody threw something at him. He quickly grabbed his gun and almost took a shot, but then realized it was a bird with a broken wing and started laughing but not before he wiped sweat off of his forehead. He went down the ladder and made his way back downstairs.

Jones couldn't help but admire the time it took to make the inside of the house so unique. The statues, the art, and the furniture – the home was furnished with the finest things he'd had ever seen. There was nothing else to investigate. He had covered every inch of the home and found nothing.

Detective Brown kept his steps short and his pistol leading the way like a hound dog would follow a scent. He passed tools, saws, hammers, and harnesses, following the noise to another door. When he opened it, he saw a machine, an advanced cutting tool used to cut large quantities of wood. There was a piece of wood stuck in it, moving back and forth. He located the off switch and the noise stopped. He walked over to a wall and saw different types of wood, all labeled. There it was: dogwood. Further into the shop, there were rows of crosses, all designed like the ones that were used in the New York murders.

Officer Hill scanned the wall with the flashlight, looking for a light switch. He found one, flipped it, and the room lit up. He discovered the source of the noise: a heater that had been left on. He was in an office, and it looked like there had been a struggle. The phone had been ripped out of the socket, little spots of blood were splattered all over the place, and there were bullet holes in the walls and the ceiling. The desk was overturned, and paper and glass were scattered all over the floor. The filing cabinet had been knocked to the ground, probably during the struggle. Officer Hill went deeper into the mystery and the smell got stronger; he blew out of his nostrils in an effort to lessen the effect it had on him. He came upon a hallway and the light fixture above was hanging and kept flickering, making it hard for him to determine what was at the end. He was able to make out the forty-five-caliber handgun on the floor. He held his weapon now in a two handed grip in front of him the way he'd been trained to do. When he reached the end, he gagged when he saw the body of a man, lying on the floor with something rammed into his chest. Judging from the decomposition of the corpse, it had been there for several days. But he knew the face and was sure it was Frank Smalls.

Denver police were on the scene within an hour, and the Denver crime scene unit was searching for forensic evidence. The detectives knew who had done this: their killer. And now, they had a name: Travis Smalls. They stood outside the house and watched as members of the crime scene unit came out of the house with Frank Smalls' body in a black bag and put it in the back of an ambulance.

Jones said, "Officer Hill, you're sure that man in there is Travis' father?"

"I'm sure of it – that's Frank Smalls, without a doubt."

"According to the M.E he's been dead for about two to three weeks, so Travis must have come here when he escaped and killed him. We need to talk to the therapist now. Where can we find her?"

Officer Hill looked at his watch. "She should be in the mountains; it's still early."

"White Stead Mental Facility?"

"Yes, sir."

"Then that's our next stop."

—

Chapter 30

White Stead Mental Facility

Deep in the mountains of San Juan, Colorado the ride into the mountains was rough and bumpy. The further they went up, the worse the terrain, but the Bronco handled well. It took almost two hours to get to their destination, but they finally arrived.

There wasn't much security, Jones thought. With all the crazy, deranged people that occupied the space in this facility, he'd expected security to be tighter. When they came to the administration desk, the secretary was on the phone. Officer Hill tapped on her desk, and with authority, he said, "Police business. We need to talk to Dr. O'Donnell now."

The secretary looked at the three of them and paged Dr. O'Donnell without hesitation. They stood in the lobby area looking serious. Dr. O'Donnell came down and was taken aback by the expressions on their faces.

"Dr. O'Donnell, I'm Officer Hill from the Denver Police Department, and this is Detective Jones and Detective Brown from New York. They'd like to ask you some questions about Travis Smalls."

After shaking hands, Dr. O'Donnell said, "Please come up to my office."

Doctor O'Donnell's office was spacious. She sat behind a desk cluttered with papers, folders, and books and motioned for them to sit in the chairs in front of her desk.

Jones said, "I understand Travis Smalls was a patient of yours."

"Yes, he was."

"For how long, exactly?"

"Almost five years."

"What's his mental state?"

"Detective, because of patient-doctor confidentiality, I'm not at liberty to give that information."

"Doctor, I understand your position, but I'm going to ask you again, for the safety of other individuals. I need that information and I need it now, or I'll be forced to arrest you for hindering the capture of a suspected killer." He could tell the Doctor had never been in a situation like this before. Jones pointed to Officer Hill, who stood up and unclipped his handcuffs from his belt. Brown looked at Jones and saw the seriousness in his eyes, the willingness to do whatever it took to get a crazy man off the streets. The Doctor looked surprised and knew Detective Jones wasn't playing games- he was serious.

"No need for that…I believe there is a clause for times like these. I would be able to give information if there's a life to be saved." Dr. O'Donnell got up, walked over to a filing cabinet, and pulled out a folder. She sat back down and opened it. "Travis Smalls... he's a very intelligent young man. Has an I.Q. of 125. My diagnosis is schizophrenia. He has all the classic signs. He hears voices, has delusions, hallucinations, and catatonic behavior. What interested me most about Travis is the conversations where he has told me that he was being punished by God."

"Punished by God – in what way?"

"Have you gentlemen ever heard of stigmata?"

Jones had no real idea of its full meaning, but he'd heard the word before. Brown and Officer Hill just looked at Dr. O'Donnell with blank expressions.

"Travis believes he relives the crucifixion of Jesus Christ. Umm...." Dr. O'Donnell leaned up in her seat and put her elbows on her desk, wiping her forehead with her hands.

"Stigmata are bodily marks, sores, or sensations of pain in locations corresponding to the crucifixion wounds of Jesus. Reported cases of stigmata take various forms. Many show some or all of the five holy wounds that were, according to the Bible, inflicted on Jesus during his crucifixion."

Jones said, "And these five holy wounds are?"

"From what I've read, the five holy or sacred wounds of Jesus Christ were the five piercing wounds inflicted upon him during his crucifixion. The first two of them were through the hands or the lower wrists, between the radius and ulna. These were the nails of the horizontal beam. The second two were through the feet, where the nails passed through to the vertical beam. The fifth and final wound was in the chest of Jesus. According to the New Testament, his body was pierced by a lance in order to be sure that he was dead."

Jones said, "So, what form is Travis showing?"

"The invisible form."

Jones repeated, "The invisible form?"

"Let me explain. I've read that some stigmatics claim to feel the pain of wounds with no external marks; these are referred to as invisible stigmata. I was working late one night and an attendant came to my office screaming I had to see something—that Travis was in some sort of trance. I went with her and whether what I saw was real or not real I couldn't really say. Travis was physically, I mean he was standing vertically and his arms were horizontal." Dr. O'Donnell showed the detectives by standing and holding out her arms, then she sat back down.

"Then he fell to the floor screaming, when he saw us he charged at us, good thing I called two attendants to meet us at his room. He was sedated; an hour later he was calm but still agitated. I asked him could he describe what he was seeing, did he remember how he came to be in restraints. He told me it starts with a dream, a vision. Having observed him in that capacity I can say it looked as if he was truly in pain."

"What's the dream, the vision?"

"All he remembers is being whipped, strapped to a cross and then he awakes in pain."

Jones said, "Travis is wanted in New York for questioning in the murders of one male and three females. The information I've gathered since my arrival leads me to believe he's the killer in New York City I'm looking for. The three female victims have all been put on crosses made of dogwood, and have been cut from the neck down to their bellybuttons and across the arms. The mutilation resembles a cross; it appears that he may have been kneeling down in front of his victims praying, maybe taking blood from them. The fourth victim, we believe, was killed trying to protect one of the women."

"Oh, my God. I would have never thought that his schizophrenia would have led him to this, even after he killed Steven. He never once showed any indication that he would kill again, never once after he killed his mother in a psychotic rage. But this is beyond what I would have ever imagined."

"Is there anything else you can tell us?"

"Travis told me when he killed his mother that God told Travis he had to serve Him or He would punish him for that sin. That he takes the death of Jesus in vain. During my research, I found that individuals who have obtained the stigmata are often described as ecstatic. At the time of receiving the stigmata, they are overwhelmed with emotion. Bearing the emotion of guilt for killing his mother may be the trigger that brings Travis to commit these violent actions. Blood, which stigmatics believe to be a combination of Christ's blood and their own, supposedly pours from the individual's wounds for unspecified amounts of time, then suddenly dries up, and the wound is healed."

"So, he's compensating by using his victims' blood to fulfill what he believes?"

"Not to fulfill what he believes, but to fulfill his delusion. I believe after Travis killed his mother, guilt came crashing down on him so hard that the hallucination of God came. This, in turn, flared his delusions of hearing the voice of God, which prompted him to believe he suffers from stigmata. Remember, all of this is in his head. Keep in mind, because Travis is so intelligent, his schizophrenia makes him a formidable foe. He'll take chances, but will be very cautious. Eluding the authorities would be something he could master, so I would say he's extremely dangerous to others, as you know, and to himself."

"Would you know anything about the dogwood?"

"I heard Travis mention it several times in our sessions, his father was infatuated with it. He was infatuated with everything about Jesus. My understanding was he did a lot of research on him."

"Did he mention why?"

"No"

"Why do you believe he killed his father?"

"His father? I didn't know he'd done that. When did this happen?"

"We found him today; Travis must have murdered him the day he escaped from here. The medical examiner puts time of death at least two weeks ago."

"His father was the one who committed him. Revenge would be the best motive. Frank Smalls never once visited Travis. I would say he had disowned his son because of his wife's death. It helped him, mentally, to dissociate Travis from his life.

Keep in mind, Travis will probably kill anything that gets in his way and twist it into part of his psychosis."

"Not if I can help it."

Chapter 31

THE ESCAPE - WHY HAS THOU FORSAKEN ME?

The Pathfinder took the roads well, although visibility wasn't very clear. The snow blew against the windshield constantly, and the wiper blades couldn't wipe it off fast enough to keep the windshield clear for even a second. He made it to the highway and gunned it. He'd been in isolation for five years, so being free now felt good. Now, it was time to make his father pay for betraying him.

"You can't trust your father, Travis"

"I know."

"You must sacrifice your father for Me and kill him for betraying you."

"I will."

Travis knew it would be a while before the attendants in the facility would notice he was gone. And it would take time for the authorities to gather men for the manhunt so he used the time wisely to pay his father a visit.

Travis switched off the Pathfinder's headlights as he parked in front of the entrance to his father's property. He got out, ducked under the chain, and made his way to the house.

Home sweet home, he thought. His father's Ford pickup was parked in the driveway. He knocked on the door, but no one answered, so he went around the back of the house and entered through the unlocked backdoor. He made his way to his room, and the sight of it made him angry. He found it empty and all his things gone, like he had never even existed.

"Kill him for this, Travis, and I won't punish you."

Travis made his way to the master bedroom; his father's room. He took off the uniform and went to the long dresser. He opened drawers and found a blue flannel shirt, blue jeans, and socks. He found a heavy black coat and a pair of boots and put them on. Then started his search for his father, he wasn't in the house.

Travis opened up the front door and saw tracks in the snow leading to the church, so he followed them all the way down to the office door. He walked down the steps and heard his father shuffling papers.

"Hello, Father."

Startled, Frank dropped the folder of documents on the floor and paper scattered. He looked frightened when he saw his son, dressed in his own clothes. He hadn't seen Travis since Travis had killed his own mother. His voice shook when he spoke. "Travis, how did you get here?"

"Kill him, kill him now."

"Why didn't you come and see me, Father?"

Frank slowly put his right hand under the desk, trying to get to the bottom drawer to pull out his pistol. "I was coming to see you, son. I've been busy trying to get things together, making arrangements for your arrival. The question is, how did you get out of White Stead?"

"Aren't you happy I'm home, Father?"

Obviously nervous.

"Yes, of course, but you're sick, Travis, and you need to be in the hospital."

Frank went for the phone with his left hand. Travis grabbed the phone first, pulled it out of the wall, and it fell to the floor. A heavy, wooden paperweight also fell. With his right hand, Frank brought up a forty-five caliber and took a shot. His hand jerked backed when he pulled the trigger. The small burst of flame was visible, and the sound of the gunshot leaving the muzzle echoed off the walls, making a ringing sound. Travis leaned to his left, and the bullet hit the wall. He grabbed Frank's right wrist and pulled him forward and over the desk. The desk followed Frank's momentum and fell to the floor. They struggled as Frank kept shooting, the sound of the bullets hitting the walls sounded like an automatic nail gun on sheet rock. They crashed into the filing cabinet, and it fell to the floor with them on top of it. Travis grabbed his father by the throat, choking him, causing Frank to nearly lose consciousness. Travis was able to stand up with Frank's neck in his grip. He threw Frank into the wall and the forty-five flew out of his hand. It bounced down the hallway, and a single shot hit the light fixture above before it came to a stop. Frank was on all fours now, making his way toward the gun. Travis slowly walked over to him.

"You didn't believe me, Father. Mother had to be sacrificed. The pain I don't deserve, she deserved it. I killed her with God's permission."

Frank rammed himself into Travis's waist and tried to pick him up to slam him onto the floor, but he couldn't budge him. Travis came down with his elbow and hit Frank in the back. Frank moaned slightly and fell to the floor face-first, busting his chin open. Blood squirted out onto the floor.

"Kill him, now, before I punish you."

Travis grabbed Frank by his shirt and dragged him over to where the wooden paperweight had fallen, leaving a trail of blood. Travis picked up the paperweight and turned Frank over.

Frank looked into his eyes. "You're the devil."

"No, I serve God." Travis said with a crazed expression on his face.

Travis jammed the paperweight into Frank's chest. With both of his hands, Frank tried to hold back Travis' arm, but it was no use. The paperweight slowly entered Frank's chest, ripping though the skin and breaking through his thoracic cage. Frank yelled in pain, while blood slowly ran out of his chest, like water making its way into a drain.

"Ahhhhhh..."

"Do you see now? Do you feel the pain? Now, you feel the pain I felt. The pain I'm cursed with. No longer will you take Jesus' death in vain." Travis kept pushing, and when it hit the sternum, Frank gasped and the last breath of air left his body.

Travis went back into the sanctuary, and in a fit of rage, he snatched the life-sized cross off the wall. With his bare hands, he pried the figure of Jesus off the cross. The statue crashed onto the floor. He took the cross and cracked it into two pieces over the podium.

He left the church, headed back to the house, and made his way into his father's home office. A rug covered a floor safe near the desk where his father kept money and other valuables. Travis opened it with the combination he'd known since childhood, took the contents, closed it, and covered it back up.

On his father's desk was a piece of paper. He glanced at it, and then God told him to memorize it, so he did. God also told him to drive the Pathfinder to the edge of the property to bypass the chained driveway, go behind the woodshop, and load up what he would need for his next task. Several minutes later, his work complete, Travis drove the Pathfinder off his family's property and disappeared into the night. He had made a clean getaway, but he had trouble maintaining his train of thought, due to the persistent voice...

"Travis...Travis...Travis."

—

Chapter 32

THE NEWS CONFERENCE

Tuesday morning. Lying in his bed on his stomach, Detective Jones used his left hand to stop the alarm clock from buzzing. The trip back from Denver had taken a lot out of him and Brown. They caught the last plane of the evening to make sure they would be back in time to start their search early.

He looked over to his right and saw Tamera sleeping peacefully. While he had trouble sleeping the last few days, Tamera slept like a log. He got up and went into the bathroom, took a shower, and then made his way into the kitchen. He turned on the TV, got the Captain Crunch from the top of the refrigerator and the milk from inside, snagged a bowl from the dishwasher, and sat down and made a bowl. After he finished eating, he went into the bedroom and put on a pair of blue jeans, a navy blue shirt, a black blazer, and his North Face coat. He grabbed his guns and badge, left the house, and drove his Tahoe to the precinct. He pulled up at 4:33 a.m., Brown right behind him in a 2008 black Dodge Charger. Jones rolled down the window, and Brown said, "Good morning, partner."

"Morning…how did you get the Dodge?"

"That Crown Vic was old. I told those guys down in maintenance we needed a new cruiser. The next Dodge Charger that comes in, call me up, and presto. Did you get any sleep?"

"Not enough. Did you pick up any coffee?"

Getting out the Dodge, Brown said, "You know I did."

He reached into the vehicle, pulled out a cardboard tray with two cups and a bag of doughnuts, and said, "So, where do you want to start this morning?"

"Brief the Captain and follow up on material we brought back. Maybe there's something in the computer."

Brown was about to respond but was interrupted by Jones's phone ringing. Jones saw it was Tamera. "Brown, I'll see you in the pit. Let me take this."

"All right, see you inside," Brown said as he walked ahead of him and entered the stairwell leading up to the pit.

"Hello."

"Hey, baby, you didn't say 'bye to me this morning. You came in late last night."

"I'm sorry. I had to be in early and didn't want to wake you. Found some information that's really helpful to my case yesterday. I'm at the station now, getting ready to put it to use, so I'll call you later, ok?"

"Jordan, I want to tell you something."

Going up the stairs and walking into the pit, he asked, "Can it wait? I'll call you when I get a chance, ok, baby? I got to go."

"Ok, call me."

"I will."

Jones stopped a uniformed officer and gave him his keys. He instructed him to go to his Tahoe and take the computer equipment inside to Larry. He saw Brown writing at his desk, so he walked over to his desk, took off his coat, and sat down. He pulled out a folder from a stack concerning different cases. Looking them over, he knew he had other cases, but this one took priority. He decided to put the folders back and write up his report of the latest events.

When the Captain came in, Jones went into his office with Brown right behind him. Captain Moore took off his coat and hung it on a hook near the door. He picked up his cup of coffee, and Jones told him what they found in Denver and who was their prime suspect. Then, his phone started ringing again. He thought it was Tamera until he checked the display.

"It's Torres." He said aloud.

Captain Moore said, "Answer it."

"Hello, Detective Jones."

"Detective, this is Torres. I just got a call. The killer struck again."

"Where?"

Captain Moore and Brown looked at Jones in anticipation; from the look on Jones face they knew the call could only mean one thing.

Another body had been found.

Torres said "Got a pen handy?"

Jones reached over Captains Moore's desk and pull a pen from a New York Giants coffee cup. He looked at both men and said in a whisper "Another body."

Focusing his attention back to Torres he said. "Thanks for the call I'll be there in a few"

Chapter 33

—

Gated Community

5:45 am. The Park Slope townhouse in the gated community was probably worth somewhere in the upper two hundred thousands. It was surrounded with police cars, police officers, crime scene investigators and onlookers. Torres was already at the scene with her unit, and Sergeant Morrison was delegating, when the detectives pulled up in the Dodge. They exited the car, showed their badges, and gained access to the crime scene. Two police officers held up the yellow tape as the detectives ducked under. The taller officer said, "First floor."

Jones replied, "Thanks." They walked into the house and spotted Torres, who was dressed in her blue uniform and had her hair up in a ponytail. When she turned around, she saw the detectives and said, "Over here."

They followed her into the dining room area and saw the victim, just like the others: dead on a cross. As Torres spoke, a man ran into the house, screaming. Brown was able to grab him before he entered the area, and Jones helped him hold him back. A news reporter and her cameraman made it in and were able to get a short video feed of the body before police officers could pull them both back. Jones went to the cameraman and took the videotape out of the camera. He told them that he would arrest them for interrupting an ongoing investigation if they didn't leave the scene. Somebody had leaked this information to the media Jones thought, had to be, one newscaster, one cameraman. What a coincidence. It could have been anybody at this point, Torres, me… myself, Brown, Captain Moore. Through updates of current events anyone could have access to this information.

Jones went into the living area, where Brown was sitting on the couch with the man, who was crying. Brown muttered that he was the victim's husband and he'd gotten away from police at the door, only to collapse when he'd seen his wife's body. Jones and Brown pulled him to the side and started routine questioning.

Torres and her unit gathered all the evidence they could, and then her crew put the victim into a body bag and transported it out to the coroner's truck. The victim's husband saw them bringing his wife out, and he started crying again. He was falling all over the detectives, they tried to console him, but it was no use. They left the house, and Brown escorted him to a waiting cruiser that would take him down to the precinct for further questioning.

Outside, the coroner's truck was blocked by a news van. The newscaster leapt out of the van with her cameraman and attempted to cross the yellow tape sectioning off the crime scene. She was stopped by police officers and told to back up. Officers yelled to move the van out of the way so the coroner's truck could pass. One of the officers went to tell the detectives a newscaster wanted to talk to whomever was in charge of the investigation, Jones came out of the house and walked over to the newscaster. He told her that he had information on a possible suspect in this murder, but if she wanted to know that information, she needed to set up a live broadcast. She agreed that in three hours she and her news crew would be in front of the Eighty-Fourth Precinct, ready for the news conference. She and the crew finally left the scene, and the detectives were able to wrap everything up and head back to the precinct.

When Jones briefed the Captain, he understood the need to use the media now. Jones worked on preparing his statement until it was time for the interview.

Chapter 34

—

THE MEDIA

The cameraman said, "We're live in three...two...one...now."

The newscaster said, "I'm Cheryl Muhammad and we're live in front of the Eighty-Fourth Precinct. Earlier today, Sharon Rosado, who resided in Park Slope, Brooklyn, was found brutally murdered in her home. Detective Jordan Jones has information on a possible suspect."

As the newscaster put her microphone to his mouth, he held up the photo of Travis and said, "This man, Travis Smalls, is wanted for questioning in the Rosado murder. If you see him, please call the police. Do not attempt to apprehend him on your own. We believe that at this time, he is in New York City. He is six feet tall and biracial. In this picture, he has a full beard, but we suspect him to have shaved." he held up another picture, a sketch of a clean-shaven Travis Smalls. "Once again, I want to emphasize that no one should try to apprehend this man. If you see him, please call the police."

Jones did what he wanted, needed-briefly- he used the media instead of the other way around. This would just flush the killer out, Jones didn't see the need to let the media or public know of the other murders or the details of Sharon Rosado murder, why cause a panic. Jones grabbed his folder and walked towards the precinct door, following him the newscaster and her camera crew tried to follow him all the way inside. They were held back by police officers guarding the entrance. The newscaster asking a barrage of questions, the sound of her voice fading, fading until she wasn't heard at all once the heavy silvery door closed behind Detective Jones. In a matter of minutes, the police department was flooded with news crews: NBC, CBS, and a host of other TV stations.

Chapter 35

—

CHEWED OUT

Minutes later, Captain Moore sat at his desk waiting, waiting, waiting; his office phone ringing off the hook. He didn't pick up right away; he gave the go ahead to get the media involved without consulting his superiors, top brass would come down hard on him for it, he savored the moment though and let it ring a few more times, then he picked up. "Hello?"

"What the fuck just happened?" the Chief of Police yelled out.

"Sir, I..." Captain Moore couldn't get a complete sentence in, holding the phone away from his ear the Chief of Police kept yelling.

"Sir..." More yelling.

"Sir, please let me explain. The situation was necessary to fan out the suspect." More yelling. "Yes sir..."- "I understand." – "yes sir." –"Ok. I will." –"yes."

Captain Moore slammed down the phone, stood up and took a look out his window and saw a mob of reporters.

The pressure was really on now and his detectives were the main targets of media frenzy.

He walked outside his office and instructed police officers to clear out the news reporters. Then walked back into his office closed his door and watched as the police officers cleared out the crowd of onlookers and pushed the large group of media personnel back. By tonight every TV station in New York City would have the photo of Travis Smalls displayed on TVs in all of the five boroughs. He would be caught- the net was wider now.

A chess move well played on his part, he made up his mind- the position of chief of police will suit him just fine- check mate will soon follow.

Chapter 36

GETTING CLOSE

Wednesday, 5:30 am. As predicted, the news had circulated the photo of Travis Smalls and it was only a matter of time. One detective sat at his desk reading the paper and Travis made the front page. The manhunt was on even more so now than ever.

6:45 am.

There were hundreds of people calling in to say they had seen Travis, but none of them had solid tips. Then, Jones was handed a sheet of paper with a telephone number. He called the number and was told Travis was staying with his grandparents. The neighbor said she knew Travis and had seen him recently, coming and going from his grandparents' home in their black van.

"Brown, it seems we've got a solid hit."

7:47 am.

Moving at speeds of up to seventy-five miles per hour, a team of highly trained SWAT officers disguised in two brown UPS postal trucks led the way to Long Island. Officers Wright and Johnson were driving a Toyota Celica, Jones and Brown rode in the Dodge. They arrived at the location mid-morning. Brown parked on the corner, and they sat and waited. Using binoculars, they were able to get a close-up of the third house from the corner in a row of five, at 1723 Green, Central Islip, Long Island, New York. Officers Wright and Johnson parked their car in front of the house. Dressed in plain clothes, they exited the car, and Wright opened the hood and tinkered with the engine. Johnson stood to the side, talking on his cell phone. The location was suburban, and the block was quiet, except for a cold, early morning wind.

Wright said into a small microphone attached to his shirt, "I don't see any movement. The drapes are blocking most of the window. From what I can see, there appears to be something flashing. There's a SUV in the driveway, though."

Jones said, "Can you see license plate?"

"No, the bushes are blocking my view."

"Is it a van?"

"No."

"Ok, hold your position."

While Brown adjusted his bulletproof vest, Jones picked up the radio and asked, "SWAT leader, are your men in position?"

The SWAT leader replied, "We're in position, and there's no movement in the back of the house."

"Locations?"

"Team one of four on rooftops, surveying the area. Team two of four covering the front, team three of four covering the back. Team four in front of the house in the UPS truck. We're ready to move on your order, sir."

One of the UPS trucks stopped across the street, and a SWAT member emerged in a brown uniform, pushing a handcart.

"Ok, on my mark we go in hard. Remember, there may be two older people in the house. Keep your eyes and ears open. Watch your fire." Jones looked at Brown. "You ready?"

Pulling the sleeve on the shotgun back and releasing a bullet into the chamber, Brown replied intensely, "I'm ready."

Jones checked his gun and at the same time they burst out of the Dodge, running toward the house with their weapons drawn. Wright and Johnson pulled out their Glocks and followed. The SWAT member tore off the brown jacket, revealing a bullet-proof vest with SWAT on it. He banged on the side of the truck, and three men jumped out of the back, dressed in black tactical uniforms, half face masks, ballistic helmets. Armed with MP5s, they rushed to the house.

"Now!" Jones shouted into his mike.

The front and backdoors were broken off their hinges simultaneously by SWAT members using battering rams. The SWAT teams swarmed the house. The SWAT leader said, "Team two up, team three down," and the men fanned out.

Brown, Wright, Johnson, and Jones entered the house. The darkness of the interior couldn't completely overtake the huge Christmas tree and its flashing lights. Jones pulled down the drapes covering the windows and light tore its way into the house, revealing a well furnished home. There were pictures everywhere. Jones walked over to one of them and saw a photo of two older people: a man and woman. The owners, he thought, and then he saw photos of Frank, his wife, and Travis smiling for the camera. He took two pictures of Travis and put them into his pocket and started searching the cleanest kitchen he'd ever seen.

Three men from team three and the SWAT leader scattered throughout the first floor, while team four stayed outside, covering the back and front of the house. Within minutes, Jones glanced out the window and saw that the whole block was covered with blue and white police cruisers. Their sirens off but their strobe lights flashing, they lit up the block like a Fourth of July fireworks show.

"Sir, all clear, but you need to come up and see this."

Jones answered, "On my way."

As he climbed up the steps, he knew what he was going to see. He wondered if anybody else felt the presence in the house, or was he the only one. A cold wind followed him, and seeped into his clothes -bone chilling- wrapping itself around his bones as if it were guiding Jones into the crypt of the dead begging him to catch the one who ended their lives.

In this suburban area, detective Jones wouldn't normally think something horrible could happen. But he'd seen this M.O. before. The open windows, the cold air in the house, the darkness, the quietness, and the eerie feeling he couldn't shake told him the killer had struck again.

When he came into a bedroom, George Smalls was lying face up with his throat cut. The blood soaked the gray sweater he was wearing. The SWAT members all checked in, confirmed the person of interest wasn't here, and the house was secure. But Jones couldn't hear them – he just looked. Vivian Smalls was strapped up to a wooden cross, just like the others, her throat cut and her body mutilated. The cross was screwed into the wall over their king-size bed. Her blood dripped down on the pillows and left stains on the fabric and headboard.

The bodies had been here for awhile.

"Nobody touch anything until Torres and her team come and do what they need to do. Brown, call it in. Make sure Torres and her unit get this."

Brown pulled out his mobile phone and made the call.

Jones earpiece went off again. "Sir, we have a crowd out here."

"Keep them back. Have the officers push all traffic back two blocks and push the onlookers back also. If they don't live on the block, get them off. If they do live on the block, they need to be in their homes."

Jones walked out of the room and put his hands on the banister, just to clear his head. He was getting angry. Angry, because he couldn't stop what had happened to these people. He took out his phone and called the Captain.

"Captain, we're too late. He's already been here. He killed his own grandparents, George and Vivian Smalls."

"It was a good call, Jones. There was nothing you could do to prevent this."

"I know, but why do I feel like I'm responsible for this? I'm going to search the house for clues to see if there's anything I can find that will give us an edge."

"Keep me posted."

Jones went into another room with Brown following him and stood in the doorway. "Brown, does anything look different in this room from the others in the house?"

"Not that I can tell," Brown said as he looked around.

"The windows, you know? They're the only windows closed throughout the house. He was here, Brown. He slept in this room."

The walls were barren, and the bed had no covers, no sheets, and no pillows. Jones walked over to the wall closet and opened it. There was nothing inside. He walked over to a wooden chair that faced the window and noticed that it was made of dogwood. He sat in it, trying to see what the killer had seen.

"Jones, what are you doing?"

"He sat here, Brown…staring out the window, thinking, maybe planning his next move."

It only took an hour and twenty minutes for Torres and her crew to make it to Long Island. When she walked into the room, she automatically said a prayer under her breath and went to work. Brown and Jones searched the rest of the house for clues, but found nothing until Brown opened the door off the kitchen that led to the two-car garage.

There was nothing that stood out; it appeared to be a common garage. There was a car parked on the opposite side of the garage, a Ford Escort. While Jones wrote down the Ford Escort's tag number, looking down on the ground he noticed there were also tire tracks on the side where Brown stood. He pointed at the tracks and Brown walked over to the garage door, he had to bend down a little and use both hands to get a good grip. When he lifted it up, the cold air rushed inside. He walked over to the Nissan Pathfinder, the vehicle Wright saw but couldn't make out the make or model and read off the Colorado license plate number. He looked at Jones "We found our getaway car."

Brown opened the doors of the vehicle and inspected it for traces of Travis. Jones followed the tracks out onto the driveway, there was another vehicle parked out there next to the Pathfinder, wide tires tracks led out into the street. Jones kept following the tracks to the street where they disappeared; he stood in the driveway of the garage and started yelling into his mike.

"Wright, Johnson, let the cruisers know I want a radius of thirty miles searching for a black van, stop every fucking black van that's seen, is that understood."

"Yes, sir."

"Brown, we may have just missed that son of a bitch. These tracks are fresh."

There was another extension to the house off the back of the garage. Brown tried to open the door, but it wouldn't budge. It took both of the detectives to break down the door. Sawdust covered the floor, and there were tools everywhere: drills, saws, cutting tools, sand paper, measuring tape, pencils, everything thing a carpenter would need. There was also a picture of George and Vivian Smalls standing in front of the Denver house, the rest of the property under construction. Jones said, "This must have been the place where Travis made some of his crosses, if not all of them."

The crime scene unit made their way down to gather evidence. Jones wanted everything that could be moved bagged and tagged. He had the cameraman take photos of the tire tracks and Travis' room and every inch of the home.

Jones instructed three cruisers to stay put, putting in the call for a twenty-four hour rotation of surveillance of the property. His request was approved.

Chapter 37

—

U.S MARSHALS

Briefing room, 12 noon. Jones took time before he went into the precinct to get some air. He welcomed the cold air pushing against his face. The faces of the dead were haunting him now, as if they were speaking to him, telling him to catch their murderer. He told Brown and the others to go ahead without him, that he'd be coming in soon, he needed to clear his head. It was better telling them that than telling them he was being haunted by ghosts.

The news that the thirty-block radius had no results, the guilt of not being able to save the Smalls, the media, everything was coming down on him all at once-pressure. The pressure was building. Being the lead detective on the case came with the burden of disappointment; until now he didn't realize what disappointment really meant. He looked up and down the block and saw people going about their lives unaware of the monster that might be knocking at their door one day. Getting close wasn't acceptable, apprehending the monster was.

The plastic Christmas tree stood in the middle of the floor, decorated with small, colorful balls and shiny streamers; there were even wrapped boxes underneath. Next to it stood Captain Moore at five feet nine inches, his broad shoulders, aging body, and salt and pepper hair reminding Jones of actor Brian Dennehy.

"Jones, Conference Room One."

When he entered the room, there were two men he didn't know talking to Brown and Captain Moore. They were dressed in blue shirts, blue pants, and tactical vests, and armed with nine millimeter Glocks. He walked over, and Captain Moore introduced them to him.

"Detective Jordan Jones, these gentlemen are U.S. Marshals Louis Wicks and William Peterson. They got here early this morning in response to Denver Police headquarters. They were notified of our interest in Travis Smalls. They, too, have been searching for him."

Both men nodded and Jones shook their hands.

Louis said, "We've been looking for Travis Smalls since his escape from the mental hospital. His escape makes him a fugitive, and we have been assigned to bring him back. He'll face charges of escape and the murder of Steven Barton. We've read over your report and I understand you've dubbed him a serial killer. Let me assure you, he's just a nut case that needs to be put back in his cage."

"I've done some research on serial killers, Marshal. I also spoke to his therapist, and I think he's more than just a nut. Have a seat, gentlemen, and let me start the briefing." Jones went into the pit, went to his desk and grabbed a folder out the top right drawer and headed back into the conference room. Pulling out two photos he held them up and said. "These two men were our first two suspects, Paul Boyd and Franklin Jefferson. Investigating further into these two men we determined they were not our guy."

Jordan pulled the wanted posters of Travis out of his folder and handed one to each man.

Captain Moore read the details aloud. "Wanted: Travis Smalls, born 1983, biracial male, six feet, one inch tall. Last known address: 11130 Antelope Road Denver, Colorado."

Jones said, "Last known dwelling, White Stead Mental Facility for the Criminally Insane. He's currently wanted in six murders." Jones went over to a projector and slid pictures of the bodies under it, and spoke as they appeared on the sixty-inch screen. One at a time he moved each picture as he spoke.

"This is what we know now. One, Vanessa Flores, Brownsville, Brooklyn; two, Pamela Washington, Bedford Stuyvesant, Brooklyn; three, Leslie Tomkins, Park Slope, Brooklyn; four, Sharon Rosado, Park Slope, Brooklyn; and five, Vivian Smalls, the suspect's grandmother.

"Three African American females, Rosado and Flores of Latino descent, they were all found dead in their homes on makeshift dogwood crosses. This wood is believed to be the wood Jesus was crucified on.

Six, Michael Weeks Jr., of uptown Manhattan. He was found dead on the floor of Leslie Tomkins' apartment. Our guess is he was killed trying to defend her. He was stabbed in the head; the knife used couldn't penetrate his skull so Travis stabbed the victim in the neck and back. Seven, George Smalls, the grandfather of the suspect, was found dead on the bedroom floor of his Long Island home he shared with his wife, Vivian. Eight, Steven Barton, found stabbed to death in the suspect's room at White Stead Mental Facility. Nine, Frank Smalls, found dead in his church office with a wooden paperweight stuck in his chest. Ten, the suspect's mother, Tiffany Smalls, was mutilated five years ago in their Denver home."

Louis and his partner cringed at the photos as they were being shown on the screen. They had no idea that the man they were tracking had morphed into such a monster.

"All of the female victims, with the exception of Tiffany Smalls, had a cross-like shape carved into their upper torso. Leather straps were used to hold them down, making it impossible for them to move. We know the suspected killer uses chloroform to render his victims unconscious.

Now, there's one piece of DNA evidence the crime scene unit collected from Leslie Tomkins' apartment. We believe during a brief struggle with our suspect, Michael Weeks grabbed at his killer's head because he had a strand of hair underneath one of his fingernails. We didn't get any hits in our database."

Jordan walked over to the map where he put red pins to mark the locations of the Brooklyn killings. "I've tried to find a link between the locations of the murders. I was trying to determine if I could pinpoint the killer's next move, but I've come up with nothing."

He pulled out another folder from his briefcase and handed detailed accounts of Dr. O'Donnell's credentials and findings on Travis to each gentleman.

"A respected therapist, Dr. Olga O'Donnell, has concluded that the suspect suffers from schizophrenia, also called dementia praecox. It is a severe mental disorder characterized by some, but not necessarily all, of the following features: emotional blunting, intellectual deterioration, social isolation, disorganized speech and behavior, delusions, and hallucinations. During Dr. O'Donnell's sessions with him, he spoke of feeling the crucifixion of Jesus Christ. She has surmised that he also believes he suffers from invisible stigmata. There are some who believe in this and others who don't. Nevertheless, it is what we believe to be at the core of his murderous behavior."

Jones pulled out another sheet of paper from the folder. He picked up a bottle of water he'd sat on the table near the projector before he started the briefing. Tightening the cap on the bottle and sitting the bottle back on the table, he spoke.

"I've been searching the internet every night looking for information to help me understand why a man or woman would kill in such a way. Of course I've heard of serial killers, we all have. But I didn't have a clear understanding as to why serial killers murder so many. Why do they kill at all? I came across Wikipedia, gentlemen; I dubbed him a serial killer because he has killed more than three women using the same methods. He fits the profile: he's murdered three or more people over a period of more than thirty days with a cooling-off period between each murder. His motivation for killing is largely based on psychological gratification.

The murders have been completed in a similar fashion and the victims have had race and gender in common. Most serial killers are not psychotic; instead, they tend to be psychopathic, meaning they suffer from a character disorder, such as Antisocial Personality Disorder. Psychopaths lack empathy and guilt, are egocentric and impulsive, and do not conform to social, moral and legal norms.

The crosses are part of a ritual of human sacrifice. Its typology closely parallels the various practices of ritual slaughters of animals and of religious sacrifices in general. Human sacrifice has been practiced in various cultures throughout history. Victims were usually ritually killed in a manner that was supposed to please or appease gods, spirits or the deceased."

He paused for a second and took another sheet of paper out of his folder.

"The mutilation of the bodies, which involves the loss of, or incapacity to use, a bodily member, is, and has been, practiced by many races with various ethnic and religious significances, and was a customary form of physical punishment, especially in cultures that embrace the principle of an eye for an eye."

Jones focused in on one of the photos of Vanessa Flores and pointed to the two spots in the puddle of her blood. He used the remote to zoom in on exactly what he wanted everybody to see. "In every murder, you'll notice these spots here; they're knee impressions. I think the killer is kneeling. He may also be praying, and he's doing something with the blood, but at this time, I have no clue as to what that is."

He stopped and pulled another sheet of paper out of the folder. "I also brought back a desktop computer from the Smalls' home and had it sent to our computer forensics expert. Maybe he'll have something for us to work on. In the meantime, there's nothing we can do but wait. The media has been alerted, as you know, and we're following up on every lead. We also handed out wanted posters to all patrol cruisers in the five boroughs. We've scheduled around-the-clock patrolling and instructed all units that if they see the suspect, they are to approach with extreme caution and take him into custody."

The U.S. Marshalls appreciated the intel. Louis said, "The house in Long Island, what did you find?"

"We found nothing that could give us a lead to his where-abouts. We did however find the vehicle he used to make his way off the White Stead property; it's being dusted for prints now. Our technicians are the best in the business- it won't take long before we have something solid."

Captain Moore stood up and buttoned his suit jacket to-gether and took the spotlight. "As I've said, Marshals, my detectives are thorough forces to be reckoned with. We here at the Eighty-Fourth are getting close, now I believe with you two assisting my men we have a much better chance at apprehending Travis Smalls, our number one prime suspect in these murders."

Louis said, "We'll do whatever we can to assist." Jones put the slide of a map he drew of the victim's residences and everything about them and all the information showed up on the huge screen. He wanted to see if anybody in the room saw a connection as to how Travis picks his victims, because he couldn't find any; nobody had any suggestions. They all just looked and listened to Jones. At that point he knew he was the leader and they looked to him for answers, it wasn't going to be the other way around.

The briefing was done-"What else was there? The Marshals had nothing to add to the case, they were just hired henchmen," Jones thought, "Muscle with guns, nothing more. Their job was to catch criminals, not to investigate them, not to look at the horror they commit, not to try and think the way they do. Captain Moore wasn't any help either, he had been transformed into a paper pusher, a fossil ready to take it to the next level, a political voice; he deserved it though, he did his stint as a street soldier, had his share of cases he had to solve." Jones admired the captain's move in taking the next step up the ladder. He gained experience, built his own list of contacts. Now it was Jones turn to grow, build, watch and learn.

The cold air in the pit was not unnoticed; bills needed to get paid. "Why the fuck won't they fix the heating system?" Jones thought, the sound of the phone disturbing his thoughts.

"Detective Jones."

"Yes."

"It's me, Larry."

"I know. Do you have good news?"

"I was able to break the encryption on the CPU and have information that might be helpful."

"We're on our way."

Chapter 38

SORTED EVIDENCE

Jones and Brown walked into the evidence room, and Larry handed Jones a folder.

He asked, "Larry, what do you have?"

"I was able to pinpoint the tire tracks to size 235/75r15. These sorts of tires are used for bigger vehicles. Vans, trucks, and in this case, I would say it was a Dodge van. I checked to see if the Smalls owned a van; they did. They also owned the Ford Escort.

The license plates to the Nissan Pathfinder were registered to Olga O'Donnell. The car was reported stolen…"

Jones cut him off. "We knew that was her vehicle. Our suspect stole it the night he escaped. Anything else?"

"I was able to break the encryption on the central processing unit. I came up with a money account. The total funds are $73,000. There are homes in Virginia and North Carolina. I've printed the addresses out for you, too. That's all the information that appears to be useful in finding your man. I've printed those documents and miscellaneous documents and put them in that box over there."

Brown went and grabbed the box.

"Anything else?"

"Both vehicles were dusted for prints and none of your previous suspects had a match. I did find something interesting – more DNA, strands of hair matching the hair found at the Tompkins, Weeks murder scene. Taken from the Pathfinder." Tell me something I didn't know you would find, Jones wanted to say, but Larry could only work with what he had, so he kept that response to himself.

"Anything else?"

"Nothing more at this time. If I find anything else, I'll give you a call."

—

Chapter 39

BACK AT THE PIT

As soon as Jones got to his desk, he called the authorities in Virginia and North Carolina. After explaining the situation to the law enforcement agencies, they sent units to the Smalls' other homes. They would call him back if they found anything. The detectives spent two hours shuffling through the paperwork Larry had for them.

Brown stood up and walked around the desk urgently. "Jones, I found something. Look at this."

Brown handed the paper to Jones, and he saw the names of the victims and their addresses. The paper had the Smalls logo on it; it also had what each individual had ordered. There were orders in Brooklyn, Queens, Manhattan, and the Bronx. There were even orders in New Jersey. The list went on and on to different states. The custom crosses were pendants made of the dogwood. Brown said, "He's following this list and killing them in this order. There are still women on this list in Brooklyn that we haven't heard anything about."

Jones called the captain and the U.S. marshals. The next name on the list was Karen Winston. Her records indicated she had no criminal history, but had a work history. Jones was able to pull a photo of her from her drivers' license. She was twenty-seven, five feet, six inches tall, Caucasian, and brunette. Her occupation was a school nurse. She resided in Brooklyn, on Gerome Avenue, near Brooklyn Marine Park. Jones called the school to see if she was at work. He was told she was out for the holidays and would return when school was back in session. He knew they had to move quickly. He couldn't wait for the Captain or the U.S. Marshals, so he grabbed his coat. "Brown, let's move."

They ran through the building and down the stairs, yelling that they were coming through. Once in the parking garage, they got into the Dodge and Brown started it up. The 6.1-liter hemi (r) v8 engine roared to life. The aluminum wheels, equipped with all-season performance tires, gripped the streets like a baseball player with his hands wrapped around a baseball bat. Its ball, the blowing of the exhaust system and the screeching of the tires, Jones used the power front seat to move up a little closer to the Glacier Magnum, a highly sophisticated industrial computer designed for public safety officials. He typed in Karen Winston's name to see if the information on the list corresponded with in the system and came up with a number and address. He called the number, and to his surprise, someone answered.

"Hello."

"Hello, is this Karen Winston?"

"Yes, it is; who is this?"

"I'm Detective Jordan Jones with the New York City Police Department."

The car glided through traffic.

"How can I help you?"

He didn't want to alarm the woman. "I'm investigating a case concerning your place of employment. I need to ask you some questions. I'm en route to your home as we speak. I would ask that you not leave until my partner and I arrive. Do you still live in Troy's Court?"

"Yes, I do."

"What building do you live in?"

"Building twelve, fourth floor, apartment 4G."

"A detective will be coming to escort you out of the building into a waiting police car in a few minutes. Until then, hold tight."

Jones made calls to the department headquarters and was connected to the nearest police station. He explained his status and situation and asked for unmarked cars to be placed in front of Karen's building until he arrived. His request was answered, and the unmarked cars were sent out.

The Dodge zipped past cars and changed lanes gracefully. Brown felt the power as he sat behind the wheel. The suspension made the car feel like they were floating in the air. They were moving so fast Brown didn't see the street name change from Flatbush Avenue to Grand Army Plaza. He turned onto Nostrand Avenue, but it was congested due to construction. Only one lane was being used. Jones showed his badge to a flagger, who radioed ahead to let his coworkers know they were coming up on the lane under construction. They made it through, and it was clear the rest of the way to Gerome Avenue.

Jones phone rang.

Louis said, "Jones, I just got your message. We're on our way."

"We're going to do things a little bit differently. You and your partner meet us at the 75th precinct. Brown and I will escort the woman back to that precinct. I have a plan."

The detectives pulled up to the building and looked up and down the block to see if there was a Dodge van anywhere. They didn't, so Brown went inside the building while Jones waited in the car. He had exposed himself on the news and didn't want to be spotted if Travis was watching.

Brown unzipped his coat, revealing his gun strapped into its holster. As he ran up the stairs, he held it in place with his right hand. His badge was pinned on the left side of his belt. Using his left hand for support, he grabbed the banister to help pull him up four flights of stairs. On the fourth floor, he found apartment 4G. He knocked on the door and Karen called out. "Hello."

"Hello, Karen Winston? I'm Detective Brown. You spoke to my partner."

Looking through the peep hole and confirming Detective's Browns badge she opened the door. Detective Brown stood moving his head back and forth. Then he looked straight forward at Karen Winston.

"Are you ready?"

"Yes. What is this all about?" Karen asked as she zipped up her coat nervously.

"Everything will be explained to you in the car. Please come with me."

Brown grabbed her elbow and escorted Karen down the stairs.

When Brown emerged with Karen, he walked her over to the Dodge. She was wrapped up in a scarf with her face covered. Brown told her to do that. So far, so good, Jones thought. After they'd gotten into the car, Brown took off. All four unmarked cars stayed in place.

Jones turned around to introduce himself as Karen revealed her face. She was beautiful, with smooth white skin, dimples, and brown hair that fell past her shoulders. "I'm Detective Jones. We have reason to believe your life may be in danger."

Her facial expression changed from curious to frightened. She pushed her hair away from her face. "Why…I didn't do anything to anybody." Her hands shook, and her eyes started to produce tears.

Jones held up a copy he made of the order form Brown had come across. "I need you to listen to me. You ordered a cross from a woodshop in Denver Colorado, correct?"

"Yes, I did."

"Where is it?"

Karen put her hands into her shirt and pulled a chain up and over her head. She handed it to Jones.

Jones held it with both hands, observing it closely. Then, he made a call.

"Larry, it's me, Detective Jones. I need you to get some men to go down into storage and go through the property of…hold on for a second."

"Karen, do you have the packaging slip or receipt that came with this?"

"No, I don't."

"Larry."

Larry put down his pizza after taking a bite. He paused an X-rated movie he had playing on his computer. He wiped crumbs off his face and pushed a button on the phone to take Jones off the speaker. Larry picked up the receiver. "Yes?"

"I need someone to go down and go through the property of one, Vanessa Flores, two, Pamela Washington, three, Leslie Tomkins, and four, Sharon Rosado. Tell them to look for a small cross made out of wood. Bag and tag them."

"Will do."

Brown pulled into the parking lot of the 75th police station, got out, and opened the back door. The detectives looked around with their right hands on their firearms in their unsnapped holsters. Karen exited, and they escorted her into the station. The Captain greeted them as they came in and spoke to Jones while Brown sat patiently with Karen. A tall white man dressed in a white uniform shirt decorated with rank, the Captain's badge shone like a brand new, freshly waxed car. His blue uniform pants were sharply pressed, and his shoes looked like a carefully buffed floor.

"Detective, I'm Captain Vega. My detectives, officers, and I are at your disposal. How can we help?"

"I need an area map of Troy's Court."

"We have a command center. In that room over there, he pointed to a room with double doors; we have the capability to view aerial satellite images of the whole borough. We can isolate that area and work on a plan."

"Good. I will also need schematics of Karen's building."

"Done." Captain Vega said as he opened the double doors.

Entering the command center, Jones was surprised at the high-tech equipment it had. The place looked like a command center on an intergalactic starship. The U.S. Marshals arrived at the command center and took a seat while Jones looked over the viewing screen. Captain Vega gave commands like he was commanding a U.S. Navy battleship; he stood with his arms behind his back barking orders with ease.

Captain Moore walked in, took off his coat, and laid it down on a chair. He shook hands with Captain Vega and took his place next to Jones.

"Jones, where are we?"

"We just picked up Karen Winston. She's ok. Brown is with her. "

Pointing to the screen, "We have the apartment building under surveillance right now with two units each…here, here, here, and here, covering both the southeast and southwest ends of the block. I also have a unit in the park, and units covering the northwest and northeast ends. This is what I need, Captain Vega. We're going to send a decoy in place of Karen Winston. At this point, I'm assuming the suspect hasn't been following her. We set up snipers here and here. There's a vacant apartment on the second floor where we can set up video surveillance."

Captain Vega said, "We can make that happen. I can have the equipment ready in thirty minutes. And men in those locations within thirty minutes."

Taking a photo of the suspect out of his folder, Jones handed it to Captain Vega. "This is our guy. Have copies made and distributed. I want a five-block radius, so we'll add units here, here, here, and here, one car on each block, just to be safe."

Captain Vega said, "Done."

Standing looking at photos of female police officers detective Jones found an Officer Burrell who resembled Karen Winston. He had Captain Vega call her in so he could brief her.

Chapter 40

—

CATCHING A KILLER

Within two hours, the decoy was in place at Karen's apartment. The units were in place, and the net was set. A U-Haul truck pulled up in front of the apartment building, and undercover officers, posing as movers, started unloading the boxes that were packed with video surveillance equipment. Brown posed as the new resident, instructing the movers; his job was to place the equipment in the vacant apartment. Using a wireless connection, he would soon have the equipment connected to small high definition remote cameras carefully placed in Karen's apartment.

Captain Moore and Detective Jones were in a van outfitted with the latest technology. Parked three blocks down, they would also be connected to the cameras via the secured wireless network. Jones sat with earphones to his ears, listening and instructing everyone through a small microphone attached to his shirt. "Marshals, are you in place?"

Louis said, "We're set."

"Units one through twelve, are you set?"

One at a time, they all confirmed they were ready.

"Brown, how's the rest of the set-up going?"

"I'm connecting the last of the cables now; I should be ready in five."

"Officer Burrell, how are you doing?"

"I'm in the apartment, cameras are up, I checked all the rooms. There's nobody inside. I'm clear."

"Ok, people keep your eyes and ears open. We're looking for a black Dodge van, run the plates on all motor vehicles fitting that description. Do not, I repeat, do not approach the vehicle. This is it...now, we wait."

"Jones, it's me, Brown. The network is up. We're live."

"Ten-four."

Brown sat on the floor in the empty living room, watching Officer Burrell's every movement. He pulled out the extra gun from his ankle holster and took it apart. He then pulled a piece of cloth from his back pocket and wiped off the outside of the pistol. Bored, he took his weapon apart and started carefully cleaning each piece of it, shifting his concentration to focus solely on his gun.

—

Chapter 41

JUST AFTER MIDNIGHT

"This is unit one. We have a van entering the grid."

"Run the plate."

"Unable, sir, it's too dark for me to see it from my location."

"Eyes in the sky, can any of you make a positive I.D. on the driver?"

"No, sir, it's too dark."

"Let the vehicle enter the grid fully. If he's our man, he'll stop. Everybody stay on point. Burrell, you there?"

"Yes, I'm here."

"Stay alert...this may be our guy. Stay away from the windows."

"Brown?"

Silence.

"BROWN?"

"Yeah...I'm here."

"You awake in there?"

"I'm awake."

"We have a black van making its way up the grid."

The van entered the grid's target area and parked across the street on the corner under a tree. Nobody could get a positive I.D. on the driver. The man exited the van, went to the back, opened the double doors, and went inside. Jones grabbed the binoculars and tried to figure out what he was doing, but he couldn't see anything.

Brown got up from the floor and went to the window. He slowly moved the blinds apart and took a peek through the small crack.

"Jones?"

"Yeah."

"I have a view of the possible perp. He's wearing all black, no coat, looks like he's wearing overalls."

"We're watching him, but nobody else can get a positive I.D. The lighting is bad and the tree is obscuring our view. What is he doing?"

"He's behind the van now. He opened the doors. I'm waiting for him to come back from behind the van."

When the man emerged, he was carrying something about six feet long. He walked across the street and looked up at Karen's window. Brown said, "It's him...It's him."

Jones gave the order and the whole area lit up like the fourth of July with sirens and lights. The U.S. Marshals, undercover men, and uniformed officers jumped out of their vehicles and moved in on Travis, surrounding him with their guns drawn. SWAT came out of the park dressed in black with their MP5s aimed at Travis. Everybody was yelling at him to get on the ground. He didn't run, he didn't move; he just stood there.

Jones ran up behind him, put the muzzle of his gun on the back of his head, and knocked him to his knees, pushing his whole body to the ground. "Got you mother fucker." He stuck his knee in his back and put his gun in his holster while the whole team of police officers trained their weapons on Travis. Then, Jones handcuffed him, hauled him up, and put him into a waiting police cruiser. Two police officers stood guard, watching him intensely with their hands on their service revolvers.

People were now looking out their windows, opening their doors, standing outside, and watching the scene. Using plastic gloves, two police officers were instructed to pick up the unassembled cross and put it into a large, clear plastic bag. The wood was still closed like a large case. Jones remembered what Larry said, that it was constructed to fold, to be easily carried. Straining, the officers lifted the wood into the back of the surveillance van.

They took Travis to the Eighty-Fourth Precinct and put him in a cell. As a precaution, Jones put him on suicide watch. Chained from his hands down to his ankles, Travis sat quietly on the steel bed frame, observing the two officers watching him. Both of them were huge men, young and white, one sporting a crew cut and the other had a neat haircut. Travis looked around the cell, and being in captivity reminded him of his padded room at White Stead. He had been free, and freedom was something he wanted again.

After waiting three hours, Brown and Jones, with the help of two other officers, escorted Travis to an interrogation room. His chains dragged on the floor as he walked awkwardly with the officers holding onto his arms. Once inside the room, he was seated. The chains that held his hands in place were fastened to a metal loop welded to the table. The chains that held his legs in place by the ankles were fastened to a metal loop welded to the floor. One of the officers stood behind Travis, and the other one stood by the door. Jones walked into the room, carrying a folder, and sat in the seat across from Travis. Jones sat quietly for ten minutes and was sizing the killer up. They both stared at each other without uttering one word. Jones spoke first.

"Do you believe in stigmata, Travis? I did some research on the issue, and personally, I think it's a bunch of crap."

Travis didn't say anything; he just looked at him. His eyes staring, wandering about the room, he was thinking of ways to escape. He lifted his hands to scratch his nose, but the chain attached to his handcuffs wouldn't allow him to do it, so he bent his head down. Then he lifted his head back up.

"Your doctor, O'Donnell, seems to believe you've been reliving the death of Jesus Christ over and over. Is that what you believe, Travis?"

"I believe that we have all sinned and must pay the price one day. But God has given me a chance to redeem myself by being his servant."

"And being his servant means killing people?"

"Those people were saved, and their blood was used to wash the pain away."

"What pain?"

"The crucifixion."

Jones sighed.

"The crucifixion." Jones repeated.

"Yes," Travis said, emotionless.

Jones leaned back into his seat and studied the killers face. No sign of remorse, no sign of compassion. He was true evil.

"Why do you believe God chose you?"

"That's beyond my comprehension. I don't ask. I just serve."

"We searched the van, Travis, and found your kill tools. The blade used in the murders will come back as the murder weapon. And we have DNA from two of the crime scenes.

You killed a lot of people, Travis. How do you feel about that?"

"I'm doing God's work."

Again emotionless, no facial expressions, no signs of remorse at all.

"God told you to kill these people?" Jones opened the folder and pulled out photos, one at a time. He said their names as he put them in order. "One, Pamela Washington, two, Vanessa Flores, three, Leslie Tompkins, and four, Sharon Rosado."

"I only followed God's list."

"You mean this list?"

Jones pulled out the piece of paper with the Smalls logo on it and pushed it closer so that Travis could see it. The names and addresses of the women on it were covered with black marker.

"Yes, that's God's list."

Looking at the list as though he could see through the black wall of ink.

"So, you are talking about this list? This is a list of people who ordered crosses from your father's business, innocent people who were killed by you. Their lives were cut short because of you."

Nothing so far seemed to even budge Travis; he didn't even blink. He was motionless.

Jones pulled out more pictures and said their names as he sorted them out. "Five, Tiffany Smalls, six, Vivian Smalls, seven, Frank Smalls, eight, George Smalls, and nine, Steven Barton. The difference is these people aren't on God's list. So, did he also tell you to kill these people?"

"It was necessary to fulfill my task."

"Necessary? Was it really necessary to kill your grandparents?"

"I myself had reservations about that, but God saw fit to do so. I was sitting in my chair, facing the window in my room. When I heard my name mentioned on the TV, I went down one flight of stairs to see you, Detective Jones, on the screen. My grandfather turned the TV down when they saw my picture. My grandfather stood up, watching the news conference, while my grandmother sat on the couch. I stood in the shadow of the stairs. They didn't see me. I wanted to just leave and finish my mission, but God saw fit to take their lives. I resisted at first, but the pain of Jesus Christ's death was too much for me to bear. When I showed myself, my grandfather quickly turned the TV off. I saw the fear in both of their eyes. They both tried to convince me that they were on my side. I knew it wasn't true, but I acted like I believed them. I went outside to prepare the van for my departure.

"When I came back into the house, I went upstairs and overheard my grandparents talking about me. When they both confirmed it was best to call the authorities, I opened their door. My grandfather went for the telephone. I killed him first. I grabbed him by his sweater, took out my blade, and cut into his neck. The blood splashed on my face. I enjoyed it, Detective. My grandmother ran to the bed, screaming. Her fear gave me more strength. She begged me not to kill her, Detective, but I was able to stop her struggle by promising I wouldn't kill her. That's the power that God has given me. I grabbed her and knocked her unconscious. I placed the cross over the bed. Then, I prepared her, and she woke up screaming as loud as she could. But nobody heard her, and I killed her. I watched her eyes go up into her head as I pushed the blade into her body. I welcomed the blood pouring out of it onto my body."

"Is God talking to you now? I think he forgot to tell you to keep your mouth shut because you just got the death penalty. You'll be in a super max until that needle is stuck in your arm. No, maybe I'll see to it that you fry." Grinning, Travis looked up at the ceiling with his hands open, fingers spread wide. Then his gaze was at eye level with Jones.

"Do you believe in God, Detective?"

"I'm a practical man."

"Then you have no faith."

"I have faith that you'll never see the light of day again. I have faith that you'll probably get the death penalty." Laughing, Travis' stare never left Jones; they looked at each other, into each others eyes.

"God watches over me, Detective. I have nothing to worry about."

"I did my homework on you, Travis." Jones said as he gathered the photos with both hands and slid them back into his folder. "And you know what I think; I think that you're just like the rest of the psychos, you're like a terrorist in a lot of ways. Always using something that was created to bring peace into the world and somehow twist it to serve your own crazy ideology." Travis balled up his hands and his fists slammed down on the table, he shouted. "NO!"

"I don't deserve this, I don't deserve this pain, I'm no terrorist! I'm a servant of God! He chooses those who will suffer, and he chooses the sinners."

"Sinners?" Jones yelled. "Were your grandparents sinners? They were just old people living, retired individuals who were just living out their lives, until a monster came out of the mist and murdered them."

"You're the reason why God told me to kill my grandparents."

"I'm the reason?"

"Yes, you put me on TV and exposed my mission to my grandparents, to the world."

"You're crazier than I thought."

"Am I, really? The Bible says an eye for an eye. The list you showed me has grown since I started with the first. I have a very good memory, Detective. All the names are in my head, and God has added a new one."

Jones leaned back in his chair and smiled. "Let me guess…me."

"No, Detective…Tamera Callaway."

Jones leaned closer to the table and stood up. "What did you just say?" Jones face became tight, nostrils flaring, his chest pushed out, his fingers looked as if they were digging into the metal table, he looked at Travis with piercing eyes. Travis was smirking now, knowing he won the battle of pushing buttons.

"Detective, surely you know who…"

Leaping over the table, Jones grabbed Travis by the neck, and started choking him. He would have surely shot him to death if he had been allowed to bring his weapon into the interrogation room with him. The two officers in the room grabbed him. Travis's face turning blue, gasping for air, smiling at the same time. Jones applied more pressure to his grip, veins in his hands projecting, the tips of his fingernails digging into the flesh. Brown burst into the room and helped to pry Jones hands off Travis' neck. It took all of them to get him out of the room.

"Who's the monster now, Detective?" Struggling with the officers and Brown, Travis yelled.

"Touch her, and I'll kill you, you goddamn psycho."

Grinning, twirling his neck, the circulation of blood flowing, moving through it again.

"Ah, Detective, thou shall not use God's name in vain."

Captain Moore said, "Jones, stand down now."

Jones still struggled with the officers a little and snatched away his arms from them.

Travis yelled, and it echoed throughout the room. "Do you know that Jesus was crucified for our sins and we take what he did for us in vain, Detective?"

Captain Moore yelled. "Put that fucking monster back in a cell, double the guard."

Brown and Jones walked out together. The two officers stood guard outside the interrogation room, and Brown said, "Jones, are you ok?" walking back and forth contemplating murder. He could think of nothing but putting a bullet into Travis's head. Brown kept talking, trying to calm Jones down. Jones finally said something.

"I'm ok. He just got to me."

"I could see that...I heard what he said about Tamera. How do you think he got that information?"

"It doesn't matter. Right now, she's safe at home, and this nut job won't see daylight again."

"You're right, he's done."

Captain Moore said, "Jones, go home and get some rest, Brown, you too. We've been through a lot these past few days. We all need a good night sleep so we can be rested for the days ahead." Brown didn't want to leave until he knew Jones wouldn't do something stupid and jeopardize the case. He needed a babysitter; he also knew he wasn't going to be the one to completely calm him down. Tamera could bring him down a notch- just enough to get him to really listen to reason. Brown said. "That's a good idea, Jones. Come on partner, let's get out of here and have a drink or something, let's celebrate. We won, Jones. It's up to the lawyers and judges now...we've done our part." Jones grinned. "You're right." Jones looked at his watch. "I'm going to go home, get some rest, it has been a long day." Jones and Brown left the station and headed to their vehicles.

Captain Moore stayed behind in his office. He opened his top desk drawer and pulled out a box of cigars. It was a time to celebrate; he took a cigar out of the box and lit it and blew the smoke out into the air and watched as the circle of smoke faded away. Knocking the ashes onto the floor and resting the cigar on the edge of his desk. He picked up his phone, made a call, and talked into the night.

Chapter 42

—

NBC/Monday Morning

Tamera didn't get up from the bed right away; she turned to look at the alarm clock and decided she would wait a little longer. Lying on her back with a pillow curled up in her arms, she stared up at the ceiling, letting her mind wander.

The alarm went off, but it didn't wake Jones. He was sleeping like a rock. He'd taken a few days off after he and Brown caught Travis Smalls. Now that the killer was caught, Jones wanted to spend quality time with his woman. Last night, Tamera and Jones had gone to the home of one of her friends for Sunday dinner. They didn't expect to stay long. But, when you're having a good time, time flies, and when they made it home, Jones hit the bed and fell fast asleep.

The flushing of the toilet and running shower water woke him up. Tamera was standing in front of the mirror, pulling off her shower cap when Jones snuck up behind her.

"I didn't know you were awake."

"I wasn't. I heard the toilet flush, and it woke me up."

"Did you get any sleep?"

"A little. I'm still exhausted, though."

Tamera turned around and put her arms around his neck.

Jones said, "I had a good time last night, though, baby."

"Is that why you feel happy?"

"No. No," he said, "This is why I feel happy." He said smiling, kissing her full breasts and caressing them. Picking her up, he sat her on the bathroom sink. He kissed her more passionately, and Tamera started kissing him back. Pulling down his pajama pants and moving closer to her. The apartment phone started ringing; he ignored it and got even closer to Tamera. Then, his mobile phone started ringing. At that point, he knew he needed to stop to answer it. Only people on the force had that number, so he slowly pulled away from Tamera. Tamera didn't want him to go, either. She was ready; she pulled him closer to her.

"Hold on, baby, let me answer that."

"No…wait. I want to tell you something."

Standing still to hear what Tamera had to say, but still anxious to answer his phone.

Tamera put her hands on his chest and looked into his eyes. "I'm pregnant."

"You are?"

"Yes, I am."

He just stood there and looked at her.

"Well, are you going to say anything else?"

Picking her up by her waist, and yelling, "Baby, I'm going to be a daddy." he held Tamera close to him and started jumping up and down and screaming, "I'm having a baby! I'm having a baby!"

Then the home phone started ringing again.

"Jordan, the phone."

"Yeah...let me answer that."

He let go of Tamera, ran to the phone and picked it up.

"Jones."

"Captain."

With urgency, Captain Moore said, "Turn on the TV, channel six."

Holding the phone to his ear, walking into the living room area, Jones grabbed the remote, and turned on the flat screen to channel six. A picture of Travis Smalls in a Denver Colorado mug shot was displayed on the right side of the screen. "Travis Smalls wanted for questioning in the murder of Sharon Rosado. He is also wanted in connection to several other murders in the New York City area; those names have yet to be released. My Denver sources tell me he is also an escapee of a Denver, Colorado mental institution, where he was institutionalized for five years for killing his mother..."

Jones turned the TV off. "Captain, I'm on my way in."

"Good. And get in touch with your partner. I've been calling him all morning."

Tamera came out of the bathroom, wrapped up in a pink towel. She saw Jones getting dressed in the bedroom. "Are you going to work?"

"Yeah."

"I thought this was our week. I took extra vacation days to spend with you."

"Something came up. I'm just going to handle this quickly, and I'll be back soon."

"Want me to fix something quick to eat?"

"No, I'll pick up something on the way."

"So, what happened? You're getting dressed pretty fast."

Buttoning up his shirt, he walked over to Tamera and kissed her on the head.

"Apparently that crack reporter did a search on the guy we were looking for, and now, he's all over the news. She's giving information that we didn't want the public to know at this time. I'm going in for damage control."

"The guy you and Brown caught a few days ago?"

Straightening his tie in the mirror, he said, "Yeah."

Tamera went to the TV in the living room and turned it on. The reporter was still talking. Then the TV showed a full picture of a Denver newspaper, dated five years ago, showing a photo of Travis' face. The headline read, "Son Kills Mother in Fit of Rage."

"Travis Smalls, whose preacher father taught him the trade of carpentry and the word of God, is also wanted for the murder of his father, which occurred a few weeks ago, and the murder of Steven Barton, during Smalls' escape from the mental facility. It is said he is being held on Rikers Island in the north facility psychiatric ward."

Tamera was still standing and watching the news story when Jones came into the living room, fully dressed and armed.

"He looks creepy, baby."

"He is."

"I'm glad he's off the streets."

"Come and give me a kiss."

Tamera and Jones locked lips for six seconds.

"I'll call you later, ok."

"You better, Daddy."

"I like the sound of that." Jones left and quickly made his way into his Tahoe, put it in gear, activated the strobe lights. Checking traffic, he pulled out into the street, and got out his cell phone to call Brown.

—

Chapter 43

BROWN AND TORRES

"You like that, don't you, baby."

"Yeah, I like that."

Brown wiped away the sweat on his forehead, grabbed Torres by her waist, and slapped her buttocks. She yelled, "Don't stop, harder, harder." Torres yelled even more as Brown complied. Then there was a sigh of relief and they fell flat on the bed as one, exhausted but satisfied. Then Brown's phone rang. Torres put her hand on Brown's back as he reached over to pull his phone out of his pants, which were on the floor. He saw it was Jones's number, so he answered. "What's up, Jones?"

"Captain wants us at the Eighty-Fourth, ASAP."

"What's going on?"

"Somebody from Denver leaked info about Travis. It was all over the news a few minutes ago. And it won't be long until the media is parked out in front of the precinct looking for answers."

"I'll be there. Give me a few. Give me time to get myself together."

Brown flipped his cell phone closed, leaned over to give Torres a kiss. "Got to get myself showered and dressed."

"What happened? It's not another murder is it?" Walking away, showing his rear end, he grabbed a washcloth out of a plastic loop attached to the bathroom wall near the shower.

"No it's the media... Travis Smalls is all over the news this morning. Got to look good for the media. There's going to be a press conference, I'm sure." Torres sat up on the bed, her back against the headboard, a white pillow shielding her breasts and private parts, exposing her well-manicured toenails. She grabbed her TV remote and turned the TV on.

"I'm Cheryl Muhammad; if you're just tuning in I'm here at the Eighty-Fourth precinct. awaiting confirmation that Travis Smalls, a convicted murderer who was sentenced to a Denver Colorado state mental institution some years ago but escaped and is said to be the number one suspect in the Sharon Rosado murder has been apprehended.

"I'm awaiting the arrival of the station's Captain Moore. He is said to be here in a few moments, my sources tell me that lead Detective Jones and his partner, Detective Brown captured the suspect in the wee hours of Thursday morning. And that early Friday morning he was transferred to the high security prison, Rikers Island psychiatric ward."

Chapter 44

THE EIGHTY-FOURTH
PRECINCT PRESS CONFERENCE

Two hours later, Jones stood tired and still a little exhausted in front of the precinct. This occasion called for a suit, but he only owned one and he'd had it for about two years. Jones, pulling the collar of his black wool coat closer to his neck to block the cold air, crossed his arms in front of him and stood beside Captain Moore, who was dressed in a gray suit with a beige wool coat. Brown, as usual, had an outfit for every occasion; sharply dressed he stood proud of his capture and his career. He was happy to be standing there with Jones and Captain Moore, to be part of history. Captain Moore took the microphone. The building was surrounded with a host of news reporters.

"On behalf of the entire Eighty-Fourth precinct, I want to thank the media and the community for being patient while we hunted for the suspected killer, Travis Smalls. He is now in custody. Now, I give you the lead detective who followed up on a lead that led to the suspect's capture: Detective Jordan Jones."

Captain Moore stood back, and handed Jones the microphone. He took a deep breath and began speaking. "After receiving some vital information that identified another possible victim, my partner, Detective Maxwell Brown, and I, with the help of U.S. Marshals Louis Wicks and William Peterson, and a team of highly-trained SWAT officers and police officers, were able to capture the suspect. Early Thursday morning, at approximately twelve-thirty am, we spotted the suspect coming out of a black 2003 Dodge van. He was carrying the weapon used in the Sharon Rosado murder on his person. We arrested him, and he is being detained at Rikers Island."

N.B.C. reporter Cheryl Muhammad, who'd given the news report on channel six earlier in the morning, started asking him questions. "My sources in Denver tell me that Travis Smalls murdered Steven Barton during his escape from White Stead Mental Facility, and that he murdered his father. Will Smalls be returned to Denver to face charges of murdering those men?"

"I believe he will, because there's a pending case against him. But ultimately, that's a decision that will be made by the judges, here and in Denver."

"My sources tell me that you and your partner, Maxwell Brown, went to Denver looking to question Travis in connection with several murders here in Brooklyn. Will the names of those individuals be released to the public?"

"Excuse me, what's your name again?"

"Cheryl Muhammad."

Jones wanted to know who her contact in Denver was. He remembered that he'd told authorities there to keep this quiet until he could make sense of the whole thing. He looked over the crowd of reporters and remembered walking into the living area of his apartment and seeing the newspaper article and the picture of Travis on the TV. He replied, "At this time, that information will not be released."

"Detective Jones, why is that? What's the secrecy of that information?"

"I'm just not able to reveal that information as of yet, but I'll tell you this. We had a few leads to follow, and one of those leads led us to the Smalls residence in Denver. There have been others murders that, yes, we believe Travis is responsible for here in New York City."

"How many murders are we talking about, Detective, and what lead were you following?"

Her questions weren't hard ones, but Jones didn't want to slip up and give away any information that was vital to the conviction of Travis Smalls. He leaned over to the Captain and whispered that he needed him to end this quickly. Reporters had their ways with questions that would make a person say something he or she didn't want to say or left room for interpretation.

"At this time, I am not at liberty to say. We all want the streets of New York to be safe. One at a time, all the bad guys get caught. Travis Smalls is one of those bad guys. So whatever lead I had, it led to his capture, and at this time, that's all that matters."

Captain Moore stepped in and said, "I want to thank you all for coming down, but my detectives need to catch bad guys. Thank you very much."

Cheryl Muhammad started asking the Captain questions. "Captain Moore, there are rumors that you are putting in for chief of police." Captain Moore didn't say anything at first but if there was a time to speak up, now was as good as any.

"The rumors are true. Yes I've been thinking of the position for some time now and believe I'm the man for the job."

The news reporter's focus was now on Captain Moore; lights flashed from cameras and there were an array of questions posed at the Captain. Detectives Jones and Brown stood in the background. They were shocked at Captain Moore's announcement. Captain Moore continued, "The streets of New York City have been somewhat of a battlefield and those people who live honest lives are viewed as prey. No longer will I stand by and have my streets cluttered with criminals thinking it's ok to be hoodlums, to rob and steal and get away with it."

"They need to know the streets of New York City will be safe to walk through day or night, that's why I've decided to launch my campaign for chief of police. I've been with the New York City police department for twenty seven years and it's time I take a more important role in this administration."

—

Chapter 45

EXTRADITION

Travis stood in the courtroom and heard the charges. He didn't smile, blink or say a word. He just looked - a huge powerful man bent on destruction. He was surrounded by ten court officers, all holding their batons. Three more armed officers stood by the doors. Security was tripled due to the extremely violent nature of Travis' crimes.

The preliminary judge hearing the charges against Travis Smalls didn't even look at the man, not because he didn't see him, but because he was scared. The very sight of the man had a tremendously threatening effect to say the least.

After hours of litigation, a judge ruled that the evidence against Travis was overwhelming. Travis would be extradited to Denver to faces charges of murdering Steven Barton and Frank Smalls, as well as theft and destruction of private property. But, he would be returned to New York City to face charges of murdering Pamela Washington, Vanessa Flores, Leslie Tompkins, Sharon Rosado, Vivian Smalls, George Smalls, and Michael Weeks, Jr.

Travis was indicted on all charges; DNA samples confirmed that the strand of hair found underneath one of Michael Week's Jr.'s fingernails was, in fact, a strand of hair from Travis' head.

It was also confirmed that the weapon found on Travis was indeed the blade used to make the horrible incisions that shocked medical examiner Torres when she saw the butcher job done on the bodies.

The judge finally took a second to look at the monster. "Do you understand what's happening here?" Travis didn't say a word; he just looked, then was led out the courtroom followed by thirteen court officers.

—

Chapter 46

RIKERS ISLAND PSYCHIATRIC WARD

After being in his cell on a twenty-three hour lockdown, Travis wanted to be free. God spoke to him every day and gave him the strength he needed to get through the solitude.

Travis heard the steps of the men grow louder as they grew closer to his cell. They were grinding chains together. It reminded him of his father; the wood cutting tools made similar noises. They were at his cell now, three of them staring in. One was a big, bald-headed, clean-shaven black man in a gray uniform. His shirtsleeves were rolled up, exposing his huge biceps. Around his neck, he wore a gold chain with the letter T on it. He opened the cell.

"On your feet," he said as he walked into the cell and stood to the right.

Louis Wicks and William Peterson walked into the cell. William had the chains, and Louis had the cuffs. They wore blue uniforms with "U.S. Marshal" written under a star on the right side of their shirts, as well as black leather gloves and black boots for rough terrain. Travis stood towering over the three men.

Louis said, "You're going back to Denver, boy. Hold out your hands." He put the handcuffs on Travis and backed up.

William took one end of the chain and connected it to Travis' handcuffs. The other end of the chain had ankle cuffs. William bent down and secured Travis' ankles. The middle of the chain had an extra length of chain, which William wrapped around Travis' waist. He pulled out a lock from his pocket and used it to secure the waist chain. The prison guard left the cell, and the U.S. Marshals followed with Travis. Travis had been housed in the last cell of eight. He looked into the other cells as they all walked towards the main gate. It took close to an hour before they made it outside.

William opened the back passenger door of the black Suburban and Louis escorted Travis inside. "Have a seat. We have a long ride ahead of us."

Louis put Travis' seatbelt on and made sure his cuffs and ankle chains were secure.

"I'll go inside and get our weapons and vests and the rest of the paperwork," William said as he walked back into the building.

Louis stood outside, keeping a close eye on Travis. When William came back, he handed Louis his gun and vest. Louis put them in their rightful places and sat beside Travis in the Suburban, Travis's body mass and huge frame looked un-comfortable, his knees pressing up against the back of the driver's seat. William wanted to take a flight, but Louis always wanted to drive. He felt it was a safety issue since 9/11, and transferring inmates on a plane could be dangerous. They drove out of the security of Rikers Island and made their way onto the Rikers Island Bridge. They drove through Astoria, Queens quietly. After fourteen hours and 852 miles of driving, they were in Illinois. It was one o'clock in the morning.

—

ROADBLOCK

Travis hadn't said anything for the whole ride, but Louis and William didn't mind. They welcomed the silence, only occasionally speaking to each other. William slowed the Suburban as they came upon trees that had blown down and were blocking the road. He looked to the navigation system to find another route and a hotel.

William said, "This side road, according to the navigation system, should lead us back to the main road and the hotel should be a mile from it."

"How long will it take?"

"Eighteen minutes. I'll use the strobe lights and pick up speed. That'll cut it down."

William turned onto the road and switched on the high beams. The road was bumpier than William had expected. The Suburban bounced left and right, causing Louis to grab the overhead handle. Travis also bounced, but he couldn't hold on to anything. He just went whichever way the bounce was more powerful.

"Now, Travis, now is the time."

Travis leaned on his side, with his back on the seat and his head on the passenger side back door window. He lifted his legs up and used both feet to kick Louis' head into the opposite door's window. Louis' head broke the top of the window, shattering the glass. The bottom part stayed intact as pieces of the top were stuck into Louis' neck and blood gushed out. Travis kicked him again, breaking the bottom part and killing him instantly. William looked into the rearview mirror and saw what had happened. It distracted him and he lost control of the vehicle, hitting a ditch. Smoke whooshed out from under the Suburban's hood.

A little dazed, William went to undo his seatbelt. Travis wrapped his hands around William's neck and used the chains and handcuffs to press against William's throat. William got the seatbelt loose and grabbed his gun. He pulled it out and was able to get off two shots that went through the roof of the Suburban. But Travis was pulling too hard on the chain, and William needed both hands if he was going to save his life. His face was turning blue. He dropped the gun, but couldn't get his other hand under the chain. Travis was too strong. Travis pulled down, using all his strength and weight, and pulled William's head over the front seat, crushing his larynx and killing him.

"Now, get the keys and set yourself free."

Travis turned back to Louis' body, found the keys, and took off the chains and cuffs. There was blood all over Louis' uniform, so he took just his gun and removed William's uniform instead. Then, Travis dragged the bodies out of the Suburban and into a desolate, wooded area. He removed his orange jumpsuit, put on the uniform, and took William's badge and the money and credit cards from both Marshals' pockets. He got back into the truck and drove back towards New York.

Travis made it to Manhattan just after four o'clock in the afternoon. He was exhausted from the drive, but God wanted him to continue, so he did. Using the Suburban's emergency lights to clear his way, he drove to his grandparents' house in Long Island. He rode up and down the cul-de-sac twice to make sure there were no police present. Then, he drove in front of the house, which was still wrapped in yellow caution tape. He needed to make a new cross in his grandfather's workshop. This one would be special.

—

DINNER RESERVATIONS

Jones was sitting on a beige leather couch in Café Remy, one of the hottest nightspots in Brooklyn. This was his way of making up for lost time with Tamera and celebrating the fact that they were having a baby. They sat near the window and sipped on drinks, non-alcoholic, of course, at least for Tamera. Jones was drinking a Corona and eating breadsticks from a bowl on the table.

Jones looked at the red dress Tamera wore – it was stunning. He wasn't good with name brands, but she was smoking hot. Her lipstick was red; her hair fell down to the middle of her back with curls on the ends. Her smile lit up the room; the black heels she wore were hot, too. His baby was the sexiest woman in the spot tonight. To her surprise, a few diners remembered her from a book signing she'd done not far from the café. They came over and expressed their satisfaction with her good craftsmanship and wished her well in her endeavors. She felt like a celebrity.

Tamera and Jones talked for a long time. Their first conversation was mostly about their plans for Christmas.

Their next conversation was basically about Jones' job and Tamera's career as a writer. She wanted to know what he was planning on doing within the department, moving up or staying a foot soldier. She understood his position posed a lot of danger, and his safety was especially on her mind now. A shootout he'd been involved in earlier in his career was something of a wakeup call when she remembered it. When he'd first told Tamera that story, they were just getting to know each other. At the time it was an exciting story to tell, and it made her see him as a superhero or at least a good catch. Either way, it worked. Jones got her. But she had him thinking now. He had to say she had a point. They dined and talked, and even had a chance to do a little dancing.

After four hours, they were ready to leave. Tamera waited inside while Jones went to get the truck. Parking had been terrible. He couldn't believe the amount of people that were in the place.

Despite the snow-covered sidewalks and the streets that weren't properly cleared, the Tahoe shone tonight. The tires had been shined with Black Magic, the leather interior wiped down with Gold Class cleaner and conditioner wipes, and the dashboard hit with Armor All. He tried his best to avoid the puddles, mainly because he'd spent twenty-five dollars to have the truck cleaned. The lights from the streetlamp hit the truck in a way that made it look new, thanks to a good wax job.

Jones pulled up in front of the café, and Tamera could see him from the glass doors. Jones got out, opened the passenger door, took Tamera's hand, and escorted her into the Tahoe.

The night ended with good conversation and a lot of good sex.

Chapter 48

—

MERRY CHRISTMAS

On Christmas morning, Tamera gave Jones a watch, and he gave her an engagement ring. She jumped all over him with joy and admired the ring, or the beauty of the ring, as the Zales' saleslady had put it. It was a three-quarter carat, round, solitaire diamond, cradled in an eighteen-carat white gold cathedral mounting with a platinum head. He'd spent four thousand dollars on it, or he would have when he finished making the payments on it.

Tamera and Jones went over to Brown's apartment later in the morning, and they had a good time there. Brown had been seeing Torres for longer than two days. Jones was impressed and surprised when she opened the door. Jones knew something was going on though, she was a nice girl, and Tamera liked her, too. They had to get on the road after a few hours because they promised they would spend Christmas dinner with Tamera parents. Tamera's parents were real estate investors and lived well, from what Jones been told. He'd met them before, but this was going to be his first time at their home.

Chapter 49

MILLBROOK, UPSTATE NEW YORK

The houses in the development were all big, expensive homes. The cars on the streets were Mercedes and BMWs. Jones didn't see one car older than the previous model year.

The Tahoe pulled into a stone driveway that led to a spectacular English-style home covered in stone and cedar shakes. It had obviously been built to the highest standards of craftsmanship with extraordinary attention to detail. Inside the home the place was huge: over six thousand square feet of elegant living space and rooms with twenty-foot ceilings. There was a ground floor master suite, three additional bedrooms, a large gourmet kitchen with top of the line appliances, a dining room, a media room, a paneled library, a gym, three fireplaces, a three-car garage, a wine cellar, and a pool. The house was on a secluded, private estate on six beautifully landscaped acres with far-reaching views of the surrounding countryside. After they ate, they talked for hours, and opened gifts in a room where there stood a tall Christmas tree decorated with glitter, colorful balls, stars, and shiny streamers.

When they finished, Jones decided to take a little walk to give Louis a call. He had called him twice the day before to see how the transfer of Travis to Denver Colorado had gone, but his phone had gone straight to voicemail. He walked into the library, made his call, and got his voicemail again. "This is Louis Wicks. I'm not in my office; please leave a message and I'll get back to you." Jones was now a little concerned, so he called his captain to see if he'd heard anything. His voicemail came on. He knew he was with family and friends and probably didn't hear his ringer. However, he didn't know why Louis wasn't picking up.

"Jordan?"

Jones turned around and saw it was Mr. Callaway who called his name. "Yes, sir?"

He grabbed Jones shoulder and extended his hand to him. Jones shook it and said, "Nice place you have here, Mr. Callaway."

"Thank you, son…I wanted to congratulate you again on your engagement to my daughter."

"Why, thank you, sir."

"You're a good man, I can tell, and I want to give you something for the both of you." He reached into his shirt pocket, pulled out an envelope, and handed it to him.

Jones took it. "Mr. Callaway, I…"

"Listen, don't say a word, and don't tell my daughter until you two get home."

They heard Mrs. Callaway and Tamera calling their names and saw them coming toward them. Seeing them side-by-side reminded Jones of where Tamera got her looks; her mother was beautiful.

Mrs. Callaway said, "There you two are." She walked over to Mr. Callaway, and they locked arms. Tamera went over to Jones and they all walked out together. They sat and talked for a little while longer about having a nice wedding. Well, Tamera and her mother did most of the talking, while Mr. Callaway and Jones just nodded their heads in agreement. Jones had a good time at the Callaway's home and knew this would be a Christmas he would remember.

Chapter 50

—

THE FIRST IMPACT

Jones and Tamera got into the truck and drove off of her parents' property. Jones turned on the X.M. satellite radio in the Tahoe and hit the R&B station. Relaxing, just listening to the music as they got closer to the city, Tamera leaned over as Jones was driving and showed him her engagement ring. He smiled as she admired it. Changing stations, Jones caught Neyo's "Because of You" and had started singing along when he felt the first impact as they sat at a red light.

Booooom....

Dazed and confused, Jones thought the car had exploded. Looking to his right he could see Tamera's head leaning forward, her body held in place by the seatbelt. They were covered in shrapnel-like glass. Through Tamera's window, Jones could see Travis backing up. That was the last thing he saw before he passed out.

Chapter 51

—

A NEW NAME ON THE LIST-TAMERA CALLAWAY

Travis

Travis spun the vehicle in an almost complete circle and rammed into the left side of the truck. Pushing it to the right, the vehicle came with such velocity that the impact caused a massive dent that pushed the driver's door inwards. The Tahoe looked like the result of a car bombing.

Travis exited the Suburban, a little unsteady. He regained his composure quickly and stopped to look at the mayhem he'd caused. He walked over to the Tahoe and could see that both occupants were knocked unconscious. He pulled on the passenger side door and heard the metal grind together. The door was stuck. Travis needed more force, more strength to pull open the passenger side door. His second attempt proved different. He opened the door and dragged Tamera out of the Tahoe. Pieces of glass that were on Tamera fell to the street as he dragged her out. Travis put Tamera in the Suburban, bound her legs and hands with leather straps, and gagged her mouth.

The Suburban had major damage to its front end and was dripping orange and red liquids. But it ran, so Travis got in, put it in gear, and sped off.

Tamera

She woke up in pain and dizzy, remembering the accident. Her whole body hurt. Her face was covered with cuts and bruises. Her dress was torn and she wasn't wearing any shoes. She was trying to focus on her surrounding, but her eyes weren't ready to see clearly yet. One thing she knew for sure: she wasn't in a hospital because her hands and feet were tied up. Her body shifted back and forth, and she knew she was in a moving vehicle.

Her eyes finally adjusted. She didn't know how long she'd been out, but could see it was still nighttime. She looked up and around the vehicle; she was in an SUV of some sort. She heard a voice talking but didn't hear anyone responding. The SUV was slowing down; then there was a sharp turn, and the Suburban stopped. She heard more talking, but couldn't make out what the man was saying.

She started to panic and struggled to get free. She heard the driver's door opening and closing. Then the Suburban backdoor opened, and Tamera struggled as she was pulled out of the SUV. She realized where she was, in the underground parking garage of her condo.

Jones

He woke up a little woozy and in excruciating pain. His right leg hurt the most – he could see a piece of metal stuck in it. There wasn't much blood until he pried the piece of metal out of his leg. He watched the blood as it oozed out. His door was too damaged to open. He looked to see if Tamera was all right; she was gone. Travis had taken her.

Jones reached under the passenger seat for his Beretta Bobcat and made sure it was loaded. He wished he had carried his nine-millimeter or thirty-eight, but he didn't. The Bobcat had to do. Crawling over the passenger seat he hit the ground. Damn, that hurt, he thought. He stood up and starting walking, limping, to be exact. Pulling out his cell phone, he called 911.

"911. What's your emergency?"

He yelled into the phone, "I'm Detective Jordan Jones, badge number 1223. I'm with the New York City Police Department, Eighty-Fourth Precinct. I need a unit to go to my home, located at 4567 Bearing Street, and look for a black utility vehicle, severely damaged. Suspect driving the vehicle is Travis Smalls. He's escaped custody and has taken my fiancée."

"Hello, sir? You're breaking up…hello?"

"Goddammit…hello…hello?"

Looking at the cell phone… "Damn, no service." He shouted.

Tamera

She struggled while she lay on the floor, but knew it was no use. The bonds held her tightly, but she didn't give up. She kept trying. She knew who her kidnapper was: Travis Smalls.

"Tamera. What a lovely name. I've sacrificed many for God, but he still has not released me."

Tamera was speechless. Eyes wide, eyebrows arched, mouth open slightly, there was absolutely nothing she could do but listen to the ravings of a killer.

"The whippings have tumbled my spirit and deleted my strength. The crown of thorns gives me no room to think, and my hands are useless. I no longer walk in a straight line. I still suffer the pain of Jesus. But you're special. You were not on my list, but through Detective Jones, you've been chosen for God. Your blood may wipe my pain away forever. Tamera, did you know that Jesus died for our sins, and we take what happened to him for granted?"

Jones

He was a half a mile from the crash when he heard a car coming in his direction. He stood in its path and it stopped. The driver from the car rolled down his window and could clearly see the condition Jones was in.

"Sir, are you all right?"

Pulling his badge out. "I'm Detective Jones from the New York City Police Department."

"How can I help? Were you in an accident?"

"I need to commandeer your vehicle."

"Take my car? No sir, you may not."

Opening the man's door, Jones pointed his Bobcat in his face. The driver didn't give him any more problems. He stood to the side, and Jones drove off.

Tamera

Travis opened all the windows in the condo and set up the cross. Then he opened the terrace's sliding door and cold air rushed in. Within seconds, the cold air had overtaken the heat and claimed ownership of the place. He walked over to Tamera and picked her up from the floor. She was helpless. Her bonds were too tight, and everything she'd tried to free herself had been of no use.

Jones

The BMW Z4 Roadster 3.0i moved like a racecar. Switching lanes was easy and smooth. He was going so fast that at times it felt like the car was getting away from him. But he kept control of it; he knew where Travis was going. At least, he hoped he was on the right track. All of the killings had happened in the victims' apartments, so his guess was that's where he taken Tamera, to their condo. Using his cell phone, "Yes! Service!" He got through to Brown, explained the situation, and Brown hightailed it to the condo. He knew Brown was closer; Brown would get to her first.

Brown

When Brown got the call, he was getting ready to go out on the town. Dressed to impress, he ran out of his apartment, securing his nine-millimeter in his holster. He left without even locking the door. Nonstop, he kept running until he jumped into the Dodge and made his way to the condo. His flashing lights and siren made it easy for him to maneuver past cars and run red lights.

Tamera

Travis held Tamera in the air by the leather straps like she was slaughtered meat he was about to place on a rack over a fire. He towered over her. Tamera wanted to be strong, so when Travis looked into her eyes, she tried to stare him down, but she couldn't…his eyes were emotionless, dark, and sinister, those of a predator after its prey. Tamera's eyes showed fear and compassion, but strength was not there, and Travis knew it. He fed off of it and smiled. "God has a plan for everyone, Tamera."

Brown

He grabbed his Franchi SPAS-12 shotgun and went to the building. The glass door was closed and his attempts to force it open did not work. He let a bullet into the chamber of the shotgun, shot out the glass, and rushed in.

Jones

He took a shortcut that would cut out five minutes of travel time. He entered the one-way street, but was blocked by a garbage truck. Two men were lifting trashcans and dumping their contents into the back of the hopper. Jones backed up, tires screeching, and praying there wasn't any traffic. Traffic cleared, Jones put the car in drive and gunned it.

Brown

Brown didn't waste time waiting for the elevator; he ran up the stairs, taking three steps at a time until he reached the tenth floor. He'd only been to the condo once, so he stopped to think. He knew their condo was on the tenth floor, but which one was it?

Tamera

Travis' eyes grew more sinister. Tamera's fear was giving him power...more strength to carry out his sacrifice. Travis carried Tamera over to the cross and was about to put her on it, but he found that taking the knife and carefully putting it on her body without cutting her amused him. Tamera's eyes couldn't produce any more tears; she just looked in fear. Her mind was thinking of a million ways to escape, but her body didn't respond. She felt as if her arms were being stretched right out of their sockets.

Jones

He pulled up in front of the building, saw the Dodge, and noticed the lobby door had been shattered. He ran as fast as he could through the pieces of glass that covered the lobby floor.

He headed towards the stairs.

He was in between the first and second floors when somebody entered the stairwell. Caught off guard, he flashed his weapon and screamed, "Get on the floor, now!"

The man dropped his cup of coffee, went to his knees, and then lay on the floor in a puddle of hot coffee terrified. Jones took another look at him and realized he was a tenant in the building, so he told him to call the police and send them to 10H.

Brown

It took a minute, and then Brown remembered the condo's number: 10H. He ran through the hall, looking at the doors. Once he found it, he put his ear to the door and didn't hear anything. Everything outside the condo looked normal. He turned the doorknob, and the door didn't open. This was Travis' MO; nothing looked as it really was. They were in there. He took a step back and lifted his leg...

Chapter 52

—

THE CONFRONTATION

Travis cut off Tamera's shirt and then her bra. Tamera was helpless; there was nothing she could do to stop him. He cut off her pants with his blade, then held her high in the air with one hand and used the other hand to rip off her panties. She was naked now, cold, and shuddering. She closed her eyes. She didn't want to see what would come next, but knew she would feel the pain.

Then, the hinges on the door broke off and the door hit the floor. Brown hurried in and turned his weapon in Travis' direction, but he hesitated because he wasn't completely in position to aim, and the uniform Travis wore had caught him off guard. He'd been taught at the shooting range to focus before he shot because he might shoot an innocent bystander. For a second, he thought maybe the authorities were inside already. But it didn't take another second for him to realize it was Travis, dressed as a Marshal.

Travis dropped Tamera and threw his blade in Brown's direction; it pierced the right sleeve of Brown's suit. The momentum at which the blade came caused Brown to lose his balance, and it stuck in the wall; with Browns suit sleeve attached. Shotgun still in his right hand, Brown used his left to pull the knife out. Travis met him with a powerful blow to his face. Browns head hit the wall, he dropped the shotgun, and blood and saliva escaped his mouth. He was lightheaded and seeing double, but he was able to pull the knife out of the wall. He fell to his knees and sat there for a second. He wanted to regain self-control. He'd never been hit that hard in his life.

Travis stood over him. "How dare you interrupt God's work?" Travis picked Brown up and threw him across the room into the flat screen TV with such force that Brown broke it in half and with it crashed into the living room wall. Brown couldn't get control of his mind because his body was taking too much pain, too much punishment. There was nothing Tamera could do but watch in terror. Picking up the knife Travis walked over to Brown. He grabbed Brown by his collar.

Jones

Jones was on the tenth floor now. He ran into the condo and saw Travis holding Brown up by his collar. He had a blade in his right hand…he raised his hand and was about to end Browns life. Jones fired his Bobcat Berretta, hitting Travis in the back twice. The bullets had no effect on him, and he stuck the blade into Brown's side. Brown screamed in pain, and his eyes widened with hate. Travis pulled the blade out and was turning around to confront Jones. Jones shot at him three more times and watched as he dropped Brown and fell face-first to the floor. His body stopped moving. Brown was hurt and bleeding, but Jones couldn't help but think of his unborn child and the woman he loved, so he ran over to Tamera first. Freeing her from her restraints, she hugged him and cried uncontrollably.

"It's over baby…it's over. Put something on while I go and check Brown."

Tamera was reluctant to get up at first. Her grip on him was stopping the circulation of blood to his arms and hands. Brown was unconscious, lying near Travis, who appeared to be dead. Jones grabbed Tamera by her arms and spoke a little louder. "Tamera…listen to me. I need to see if Brown is ok, and I need you to go in the bedroom and put something on, ok, baby?"

Tamera nodded her head and then looked into his eyes. She wiped away the tears on her face. Jones saw a sense of steadiness. She was getting control of herself and realizing that he was there and that imminent danger was no longer an issue. He stood up with her and walked her to the bedroom.

Brown was slowly moving now. Jones went over to help him up, but was grabbed from behind which caught him off guard, and he dropped his weapon. Travis was still alive.

Five bullets in this monster, Jones thought. Travis swung him around and grabbed him by the neck. Jones grabbed him by his and they struggled, going around in a circle, using their strength to gain superiority. Travis' belief that he was a servant of God doomed to repeat the pain of Jesus Christ's crucifixion to absolve his sins fueled his anger and his strength. Jones's belief in the law and the need to provide safety for Tamera and his unborn child fueled his strength. Jones, twenty-eight, Travis, twenty-five, and they were the same height and of similar build. Was he his nemesis…was Jones his?

Jones leaned his head forward and rammed his forehead into Travis's. Travis showed some signs of disorientation. Jones kept ramming his head into his. Travis's eyes grew wider, a crazed look on his face, combined with a smile "Is that all you got." then he violently slammed his head into Jones'.

Heads slamming- brack, brack, brack, Jones fell to one knee, but he thought they were matched, locked into a battle that could go on for eternity. Jones reached for his Bobcat Berretta, the tips of his fingers touching the handle, but he couldn't get a firm grip on it. Travis kicked the gun further away, he could have picked it up but using his bare fists against Jones face was satisfying. Jones couldn't focus; his brain rattling inside his head, he couldn't send a complete message to his hand, his legs, he was being beat badly.

Brown was barely coming around, but he was able to get on his feet. He put his hands on his side to try to stop the flow of blood. Limping and wincing in pain, he saw the shotgun across the room, near the door, and went for it. Jones was on one knee and Travis said, "This is God's will. You cannot defeat His will, nor can you defeat me." He struck his jaw, and Jones fell to the floor. Travis saw Brown running for the shotgun and grabbed him by the arm. The shotgun lay a few feet away. Jones was wobbly and his jaw was aching, face bleeding, but he rammed himself with full body force into Travis and they all went through the open doorway onto the terrace, tussling and punching. Travis was too strong for them both; he knocked both of them to the floor. Then, there were gunshots.

Tamera looked like a female Rambo as she held the shotgun like a pro, releasing four rounds in one second. The fear in her eyes was gone, and four powerful blasts hit Travis' chest, backing him up and bringing him to his knees. Jones was sure he would be dead at that point, but he wasn't. He was hurt, though; he could see the pain in his face. Brown was unconscious and losing blood rapidly, but he was alive.

Travis was getting back up slowly; Jones and Tamera couldn't believe their eyes. Then they saw why: he had on a bulletproof vest. The impact of a shotgun with such power still should have knocked him out cold, but it hadn't.

This man just wouldn't die. Tamera pulled the sleeve of the weapon then the trigger on the shotgun, but it jammed. Travis got to his feet and headed in Tamera's direction. Jones used what strength he had left to charge at him, and they went flying over the terrace railing. Tamera yelled out Jones's name and ran to the railing. Jones was able to hold onto the bottom of the terrace floor with his right hand. Travis had a grip on his left leg. They were dangling hundreds of feet in the air.

Tamera reached out to Jones, trying to grab his hand. He lifted his right leg and kicked down hard. Travis went falling. Tamera reached out her hand to Jones. He grabbed it, and she helped pull him up and over the railing and back onto the terrace. They sat on the terrace holding each other.

Soon, the condo was overrun by uniformed police officers. Captain Moore, Sergeant Morrison, Officers Wright and Johnson were there, Brown was still unconscious, but alive for the moment, and he needed medical attention fast. Tamera was still shaken up and scared. Jones was in serious pain and just glad it was over.

When the police went down to recover Travis's body, Travis wasn't on the ground, broken into a million pieces on Christmas night. He was gone, disappeared into the night amid the darkness, the cold air, and snow.

Chapter 53

—

Six Days Had Passed

The F.B.I. and local law enforcement agencies still hadn't been able to get a lead on Travis's whereabouts yet.

The bodies of US Marshals Louis Wicks and William Peterson were found decomposing off a dirt road among trees and rocks in Illinois. Louis' neck was almost severed, and William had been asphyxiated and was wearing only his underclothes.

Travis' blade had gone deep into Brown's body, but didn't damage any internal organs. He was covered with cuts and bruises, his right eye swollen, and his right arm and ribs broken. A couple of months in the hospital and he would be ok. Torres practically moved into the hospital with him; she stayed by his side all day, every day. The question is will Brown be able to make this a long lasting relationship.

Tamera couldn't go back to their condo just yet; she probably will never go back. She stayed at her parents' home. The horrific nightmare was over for now, but the man in the nightmare was still at large. Tamera was never the same again; she was still reliving the nightmare in her dreams.

Doctors confirmed that if she didn't rest and practice stress management that she could have a miscarriage. Jones was banged up and bruised himself, but he had to catch a killer and with Brown out of commission it was up to him to do it alone.

Captain Moore was given a reprimand for his announcement on national TV that he wanted to be considered for chief of police. He was preparing his speech for his upcoming news conference. Nevertheless, he was still looking forward to becoming the next chief of police.

Chapter 54

—

THE LIST

Jones wanted revenge for what Travis put Tamera through, for hurting Brown and for all the people he killed. His black Carhartt jacket was open; leaving the bulletproof vest with his badge pinned on the left side in sight. Wearing a pair of blue jeans and a pair of six-inch black suede Timberlands, he stood in the dark, holding the same Frenchi SPAS-12 shotgun Brown had brought into the last confrontation. He waited in the apartment of Karen Winston for a week and a day. Karen and everybody else on the list had been temporarily relocated. He had a feeling that Travis would come there.

The door opened. There he stood; the light from the hallway overtook the huge outline of his body and showed a shadowy figure on the floor. When he came into the apartment, he was still wearing the US Marshal's uniform. He held a blade longer than the knives he'd used before – it was more like a sword. It was as if he knew Jones was waiting for him, and he came prepared to battle.

Jones lifted the shotgun and pulled the trigger. Travis moved about quickly, as did he, aiming the shotgun, but every shot he took missed him. Before he knew it he was in front of him, and he swung the blade and attempted to bring it down on Jones's head. He blocked it with the shotgun and was able to push Travis up against the wall. They were pushing back and forth. Jones was more focused than he had been in the condo. He was mentally ready, so his body was working with him. He was winning this time. Focusing his strength on his left arm, he forced it forward and was able to hit Travis across the face with the fore grip of the shotgun twice. The second time, blood came out of his mouth and he appeared to be a little stunned. So he did it again and again. Travis dropped the sword and stood wobbling. With both hands wrapped around the muzzle of the weapon, Jones swung the shotgun into his face. He flew onto the floor. He raised the shotgun back up to come down on his head, but Travis grabbed him by the waist and body slammed Jones onto the floor. The back of his head hit the floor hard.

Visions of ultimate fighters ran through his mind. They were two titans, using their wills to determine the outcome of the battle, knowing that only one man could win. Wrestling with each other, Jones was able to get on his feet, and they both threw punches at each other. He was catching Jones in the face, and Jones was doing the same. The living area looked as if a tornado came through it.

They were in the kitchen now, tussling, crashing into the kitchen table. Placemats and napkins fell to the floor. Jones smashed Travis's head into the refrigerator and used his elbow to pin his head up against the refrigerator door. He was dazed again, and Jones had the advantage, so he took a step back, pulled Travis's head forward and hit him in the head with his right knee. While he was falling, he jabbed him with a right hook, and he fell to the floor, hard.

Jones got on top of him, ground and pound was all he could think of, and started to pummel his face with powerful left and right punches until he stopped moving and was unconscious. Shaking, bloody, his body in pain he grabbed Travis by his collar with his left hand, stood up, and dragged his battered and beaten body out of the apartment, picking up the shotgun with his right hand on the way. Residents opened their doors and watched, whispering to each other, as he dragged him through the hallway, leaving a bloody trail.

Jones dragged him down four flights of stairs. Once he was outside the building, police cars rolled up, surrounding him. The neighbors had called in the disturbance. With what little strength he had left in his arm, he hurled Travis into the street. He took his badge off his vest.

"I'm Detective Jordan Jones, and this man is under arrest."

Four officers walked over and picked up Travis and put him up against one of several police cars that came to the scene. Jones still hurt, carrying the shotgun he walked over to Travis as his head was being pushed up against the hood of the police car. "You have the right to remain silent. Anything you say or do, you will be held accountable; you have a right to an attorney. If you cannot afford one, one will be appointed for you. Do you understand these rights as I have said them to you?"

Chapter 55

—

MONTHS LATER

People were still talking about Travis Smalls. The media had dubbed him The Cross Killer. Jones and Brown were both given medals of honor for capturing the murderer of two U.S. Marshals and for closing the biggest case in New York City. Captain Moore made sure he was in the middle of the detectives when the photo was taken of them receiving their medals. His bid for chief of police had put him in a position of a politician.

Tamera was still traumatized; the stress weighed down on her so much she miscarried. Travis was tried and convicted in New York City for all his crimes and found guilty by reason of insanity. He was sent to the Rikers Island prison ward for the criminally insane and kept under heavy sedation; he's like a zombie now.

Chapter 56

Rikers Island Hospital Prison Ward for the Criminally Insane

Travis stood next to a metal chair with black and grey paint peeling off it looking out the window of his cell wearing a white jump suit. The length of the jumpsuit pants legs were too short for his tall frame, they came just below his calves.

Travis's schizophrenia is the demon that rests inside him, trying to find its way through the drug chlorpromazine, which is used as a treatment for psychiatric disorders. His cell door opened and two armed guards accompanied by a woman entered. "Have a seat Travis," the woman said as she sat in a chair brought in by one of the armed men. Travis didn't move, he stood looking out the window, he knew the voice though- it was Dr. O'Donnell. "I came a long way to see you Travis, please have a seat." Dr. O'Donnell put her briefcase beside her on the floor and folded her arms on the metal table. Travis kept staring through the bars guarding the window, observing white birds flying around peacefully. To him they looked like angels trying to send him a message from God that he has yet to decipher.

"Doctor, do you know that Jesus died for our sins and we take what he did for granted?"

A CARTER PUBLICATION

Kids playing baseball find the body of a dead woman rotting in a ditch, after her identity is confirmed. New York City officials are shocked and want the best to solve her murder.

Jones is called back in to handle the case, higher ups at One Police Plaza think it's time to put aside the past and get back to work.

Reluctant at first, Jones decides it's time to get back also, as the story continues he is thrown back into the field of investigation. Read along as he enters into the mind of a killer that will stop at nothing to keep his secret from bringing shame to his family.

Page after page the story gets even better. The twists and turns will keep you guessing. Be on the lookout for The Cold Cases....... CHECK OUT THE PREVIEW

THE COLD CASES

A JORDAN JONES NOVEL

Edited by Shera Coleman

Chapter 1

—

NIGHTMARES

Detective Jones woke up from the same dream he'd been having for the past couple of months now, sweating, cold and shivering, unaware yet that he was still in his bed. He kept grabbing at his waist believing his gun was there. Still a little groggy, he began to realize where he was, in his bed. Then he screamed.

He was having the same dream every other night, his sleeping pattern becoming more erratic. Deep down, he knew he would probably never be the same. His first real homicide case had soured his relationship and his outlook for the job. Still, he couldn't see himself doing anything differently.

Beads of sweat covered his face and his body felt as if he'd just exited a sauna; he grabbed the top sheet from the bed, and wiped his face, leaving a small but noticeable stain. He threw the sheet to the side, placed his feet on the floor, and grabbed his Blackberry off the night table to see the time. He wasn't late yet. Getting up, he let his boxer briefs fall to the floor, walked into the bathroom and stood in front of the mirror over the sink. He ran cool water from the faucet, cupped his hands and pushed his face into the small puddle, thinking that would help pull his thoughts together. It didn't.

The warm water from the shower pulsating down his body was enough to rejuvenate him, just what he needed, he thought. He came out of the shower and stood naked in front of the dresser mirror, really noticing how well he had transformed his six-foot frame into a lean mass of defined muscle. His motivation to do so had been the intense hand-to-hand combat with a psychopath who nearly overcame him. Sheer grit and determination saved him then, but he vowed he wouldn't be put in that situation again. Since then, he had taken up kickboxing and Brazilian jujitsu. His trainers were surprised at his ability to pick up the moves and build a technique of his own. Mixed martial art was always an interest, so when an opportunity came to square off in an amateur fight, he jumped at the chance and won. As he dressed, the smell of those perfumes sitting atop the dresser filled the room, like it did every day when the steam from the shower vanished...and like always, it reminded him of Tamera. He missed her so much he could still hear her voice and smell her scent. She said she needed her space, though. He knew that, but didn't have to agree with it. He was ready for work; he grabbed his badge, guns, and phone, locked the condo, and headed down to his rental, compliments of New York's finest.

He'd been seeing a therapist for the past two weeks, and promised to call if he had the dream again. "Hello, Doctor; it happened again. The dream never changes- the first impact hit the Tahoe on the right and it slid sideways, leaving deep skid marks on the street. Both right side passenger windows exploded. The glass looked like shrapnel as it flew into our faces and necks. Shards of glass were inside and outside of the Tahoe.

The second hit came from the same vehicle. It spun in a three-sixty and rammed into the left side of the Tahoe, pushing it to the right. The vehicle driven by Travis came with such velocity that the impact caused a massive dent that pushed the right driver's side door inwards. It pushed into my right leg, slightly pinning me in. The car looked like a target from a car bombing.

Travis exited the Suburban, a little unsteady. He regained his composure quickly and stopped to look at the mayhem he caused. He walked over to the Tahoe and saw me woozy and disoriented and Tamera knocked unconscious. He pulled the passenger side door. I heard the metal grind. It was stuck. Travis put more force into his second attempt. I could see his biceps bulge and the angry intensity in his face. He finally yanked the door open and dragged Tamera out by her hair. He turned to look at me with a sinister smile. He pulled out a long sharp blade and drove it into her body. I held out my hand, screaming, no. Then, I always wake up sweating and yelling Tamera's name."

"Jordan, we know that when Travis kidnapped Tamera he didn't stab her. Your subconscious mind is holding onto a sense of guilt, making you feel responsible for things you had no control over, like not being able to save Travis' grandparents or your own unborn child. You may be harboring this and see it as a reason for the distance Tamera has put between you two. Jordan, maybe you should come into my office so that we can talk more about this."

"We've been talking about this dream for months now, Doctor, and nothing has changed. I'll call your office and set something up for next week. I'm back in rotation and due into work in ten minutes. The last thing I need is to be taking time off on my first day back because I need to see my shrink. If for some reason I need to talk more about this before then, I'll call you."

Jones thumbed the end button on his Blackberry and started to put it in his pocket but it vibrated before he could. He looked at the number displayed on the small screen-it was his partner, Maxwell Brown. He thumbed the talked button. "Jones" he answered.

"I'm at the front entrance of Prospect Park, Jones. We're up."

Chapter 2

LAST NIGHT

The weather was just right. Tracey opened the main door to her apartment building and made sure it was closed and locked. She took the stairs to her third floor apartment and got ready for her jog. She put on a white Baby Phat sweat suit, white and blue Nikes, grabbed her iPod, and made her way out into the street. Tracy stood in front of the park and lifted her legs one at a time for a good stretch and started her five mile jog through the park.

A mile into the run, a sweating, semi-exhausted Tracey stopped by a fountain and took a long draw of the water as it pushed into her mouth. She bobbed her head to the sounds of Ciara's 'Like a Boy.' Then she felt something wrap around her neck, pulling her into the wooded area behind her. Her eyes bulged from the pressure being applied, moving left to right frantically. Her mouth opened, and a light scream escaped but was immediately subdued by the force of the strap pulling down on her throat. Tracey's iPod dropped to the ground and bounced twice on the pavement before it stopped in the grass, its light still glowing in the darkness. The music could still be heard through the tiny earphone pieces.

She used both hands to pull the strap forward. She struggled with her attacker. She used her karate skills and for a few minutes, she was in control. She was able to release herself from the strap around her neck. She fought hard with the man, blocking punches, kicking to the stomach and legs. They had eye contact until he connected with a left hook, knocking out one of her front teeth, splattering blood all over her jacket. She fell to the ground hurt and dazed, but still held it together. The man stood over her. Still a little confounded, with blurry eyes and a sore bloody mouth; she was able to get in a good groin kick. He fell to his knees in pain, and then reached out to grab Tracey's leg, but she took off running through what looked like a jungle right then. She knew the jogging trails like the back of her hand but being inside the park's belly was different. How would she navigate through this? Too late for that, she figured; she would make the best of it.

Grabbing branches with precision, she ducked under and jumped over them. She wished she had a machete to cut a path straight through. She wanted to come across some life… anything to say that she wasn't alone. There was nothing… nothing but trees that stretched farther than the eye could see. She heard sirens though, and followed the sound.

She looked up into the sky and the moon's rays beaming down to the earth gave her some light. As she ran, she wondered if God was giving her a path, if this was God's light that so many people talked about. Her track suit was ripped and covered in small bloodstains, her Nikes scuffed. She wanted to scream out but knew that would only alert her pursuer to her location, so she kept quiet. When she thought she had escaped her attacker, she stopped to gather her thoughts. She heard something moving, not far from where she stood. She stayed still and tried to focus her eyes on the spot where she'd heard the movement, but it was too dark to see.

Blood kept dripping from her mouth as she took her fingers and felt the gash in her lip. She heard the movement again; he was getting closer. Thinking her position was compromised, she took off running. The leaves moving with the flow of the breeze, the crickets chirping, and all the familiar sounds seemed to be amplified a million-fold. Was it God giving her the ability to heighten her hearing, to hear what she normally wouldn't, or was it fear? Was fear heightening her senses?

He was playing with her and she knew it, like a cat playing with a mouse, the mouse knowing it had no chance of escaping. She picked up a stick and yelled, "Come on, you want me, come and get me- you motherfucker!" She held the stick in front of her, ready to swing at the man. She stood ready for combat, her black curly hair in disarray, gym suit caked in dirt, and blood dripping from her mouth,

"Come on motherfucker, I'm here! Come on, I'm ready! What are you waiting for?" she yelled as she whirled around. Then something darted from the woods - it was a dog. She wanted to laugh really, but she didn't. The dog had caught her off guard. The strap was suddenly around her neck again, the man stood tall, lifting her completely off the ground. The obstruction of blood flow to the brain produced large veined impressions that protruded from her forehead, turning her bulging eyes bloodshot. She was in his powerful grip. He pulled and pulled, choking the life out of her as she struggled, kicked and clawed until there was no life left. Her arms went limp, and her body hit the ground.

The killer walked away.

Chapter 3

—

DEAD BODY

Three police cars and Detective Brown's Dodge Charger blocked off Grand Army Plaza's entrance to the park. Two other police cars blocked off Prospect Park West and two more blocked off Eastern Parkway. No cars were allowed down those streets, so the traffic piled up on Flatbush Ave. Detective Jones leaned out the window, showed his badge and one of six officers waved him on through the blockade.

Jones parked the car and walked up to the crime scene.

The body lay sprawled in the grass under well-manicured shrubbery, her eyes open, and her head lay hanging off to the right side as if she were a ragdoll. The white jacket and pants on her body were ripped and covered in dirt and dried blood. The whites of her eyes still shined brightly. Her mouth hung open, a deep gash in her lower lip, dried blood covered it and the right side of her face was swollen and bruised. From what Jones could see, her hands had bruises on them also. She fought hard - but not hard enough, he thought.

Medical Examiner Torres stood over the body taking notes and Detective Brown stood observing the scene.

Police officers walked up and down the line of onlookers, asking them questions as they stood watching the crime scene team work. One of the C.S.I. techs walked around the body and took pictures while another combed the immediate area for trace evidence.

"Torres, how are you?"

"I'm ok, glad to see you back." They shook hands.

"Thanks."

Jones walked up to Detective Brown.

"Brown, what's up?"

"Just got here not too long ago myself. I've been calling, Man, you ok?"

"I'm ok, just needed to be alone for a few days, you know."

"Yeah, it happens."

"Six months off and already we're back in rotation. How's your side?"

"If you had asked me that question six months ago when that motherfucker stuck me, I would've said it hurts like hell. But now with the help of painkillers, it's not so bad- and the doctor didn't do a bad job of stitching me up either." Jones patted Brown on the back. "Scars make a man, at least that's what the women say. So what we got?"

"She's young for sure. Late twenties is my guess, African American obviously. No I.D. on her person," M.E. Torres said, as she knelt and pointed to her neck. "From the ligature marks on her neck, it looks like she was strangled to death."

Pointing to her hands.

"Looks like your Jane Doe put up a fight also, you see her hands; she's a puncher not a scratcher. If she were a scratcher we probably would have had some good clean DNA to look at under her nails. We still may have other DNA on her clothes or on other parts of her body, but I won't know until I get her back and autopsy the body."

"Boxer, maybe."

"Could be, but not likely; she looks kind of short for the sport. But you never know."

"How tall is she?"

"5'8", by my measurements."

"Looks like she was out jogging last night."

"That would be my guess, gym suit and all."

"How long has the body been here?"

"I can't say for sure until I get the body back, but from looking at the discoloration of her skin," Torres shrugged, "less than fifteen hours."

Brown looked at the victim's feet. "She's missing her left sneaker and her right has dirt deeply imbedded into the sole."

Jones bent down and took a pen from his shirt pocket and pushed the sneaker up a little and looked at the white ankle tube sock on her left foot. "She ran from her attacker and it ended here. From the condition of her sock on her left foot, it looks like she ran for some time. Has a patrol been sent out for evidence search?"

"Not yet."

"Who found the body?"

Brown turned around and pointed.

"Those kids over there. I had Wright and Johnson keep an eye on them; they were the first officers on the scene also. The parents just arrived a minute or two before you got here."

"Has anyone spoken to them yet?"

"No, I wanted to wait until you got here and we'd go at it together."

"Any witnesses come forward?"

"Not yet, I've got uniforms asking questions. I instructed them to let me know ASAP if anybody says they heard or saw something."

"Torres - if you're done, bag and tag. Don't want the media getting a shot of any of this. I'm surprised I haven't seen media yet."

Jones and Brown walked over to three little boys, two of them black, one white. One of the black boys was about five feet seven, the tallest of the three. He was a baby-faced kid wearing a navy blue Yankees baseball cap and a blue jacket with N.Y. embroidered on the back, blue jeans and white and blue Air Jordan's. The other black kid was shorter, five feet tall, dressed in a blue Sean John velour track suit, with all white Nike sneakers the kids call uptowns. He held a baseball in his left hand. The white kid wore blue faded jeans, a Mets baseball jersey, had a shag hairstyle, and white sneakers. He held a baseball bat in his hands. Jones and Brown walked up to the officers.

Jones said, "Wright, Johnson." Both officers nodded their heads in recognition of the detectives.

"Have any of the parents asked any questions yet?"

Officer Wright rested his right hand on his gun. "Not yet, been listening to their kids so far."

"What time did you guys get the call?"

"The call came in at... Johnson what time was that?" Johnson pulled out his pad and flipped it open. "The call came in at 8:45am and we arrived at 9:22am. Anthony Clark saw the body first." Officer Johnson pointed to the bigger kid. "He called it in to 911."

"How old is the kid?"

"Eleven."

"Big boy."

"Yeah for eleven, the smallest is his brother, and the white kid is a friend of theirs. They told us they hang out here every other day pitching and batting."

"Thanks, fella's."

The detectives walked over to the small crowd of individuals, wearing their badges at eye level. The parents of the children came at them like a swarm of bees after honey, asking a million questions. It took ten minutes to calm them all down and to reassure them that their children's involvement in the matter went no further than answering some basic, routine questions. Jones walked over to Anthony and asked him a host of questions while Brown took notes.

Anthony told Jones that he and the other two boys were hitting the ball around when his little brother hit a ball that landed in the area were they found the body. He made a point of saying it wasn't really a homerun but he's my little brother, and that they stood over the body and watched it, amazed at seeing a real dead body. Once satisfied it was real, he called 911. He knew to call 911 by watching the television show 48 Hours with his parents.

Anthony said his mom thought he was telling a lie, playing a joke, but heard the seriousness in his voice and the wailing of police sirens in the background. And that they stood and watched as a police car rolled up, and then, a few more.

"Are you gonna catch the bad guy?"

"I'll try my best to, kid."

The other boys gave the same account of what happened, except Anthony's little brother said he hit a home run. Jones thanked the boys and their parents for their patience. He turned to Officers Wright and Johnson and instructed them to gather license plate numbers from all the cars surrounding the entire block. She could have driven a car here, maybe. Having a list of license plates could be helpful once the body was identified.

Jones and Brown turned around to the sound of an ambulance backing up, sure that its loud beeping noise could be heard three blocks away. It stopped abruptly. Torres stood in back of two tall men wearing morgue jackets as they hauled the gurney with the dead body wrapped into a black body bag into the back of the ambulance. Torres walked over to the detectives.

"I'm done here; I should have the autopsy done in a day or two. I'll have her fingerprints taken and sent as soon as I get the body back to the morgue. I should have them by tomorrow afternoon at the latest. Tonight, if we're lucky."

Jones said, "Ok, we'll stick around here and see if we can find the other sneaker. Maybe we'll have a clearer scenario of what happened to our cadaver."

"I'll send you guys the results of the autopsy as soon as I get it." Jones shook M.E. Torres hand and stepped to talk to several police officers. Brown walked Torres to the ambulance, where they spoke briefly and embraced.

Torres entered the ambulance and two police officers cleared the way for the ambulance to make its way onto the street. Once cleared, the ambulance strobe lights activated with the sirens blaring and it sped off.

Chapter 4

—

EVIDENCE SEARCH

Detectives Jones and Brown, with the help of a team of uniformed police officers, set out to find the point of origin that led up to the death of the dead woman.

Jones had all the men gather around him. The police officers, all of them younger than him; the blue uniforms reminded him of when he was a uniform cop. The nights he spent in a patrol car patrolling the streets, it seemed like yesterday. The days when he'd stood before detectives, and took orders from them.

He was in that position now.

"Listen up, it appears that our victim was jogging in this park last night and at some time during that jog she was attacked and killed. Her left sneaker is missing and that tells me she was chased through the park and at some time during that chase her sneaker came off or it came off during the first attempt to take her life. Either way, that sneaker I believe is still in this park somewhere. We are looking for a white sneaker with a blue Nike sign on the sides. We'll split up in teams; we'll cover more ground that way."

Jones took a team of officers with him and headed in the direction of northwest, northeast and Brown took a team of officers and headed southwest, southeast.

Forty five minutes later.

Detective Brown stopped to take a sip of water from a fountain that sat near a bench covered with leaves; his team members, in all directions searching the grounds for the missing sneaker. As he rose something shined and caught his attention in the thick shrubbery. He walked over to the spot, and noticed the branches were broken inward and the impressions that sat deep in the dirt. Taking a deeper look, there lay an iPod; its silvery back side shined off the sun, black wire ear phones still attached to it. The sneaker wasn't far away.

He called Jones.

When Jones came over and saw the iPod he took a deeper look into the shrubbery and could see what was left of a scuffle. Large boot prints and sneaker prints all over the area. "This is the place of origin Brown." Jones knelt down on his left knee and pointed. "The struggle started here, this area right across the water fountain. She must've been taking a drink of water and the killer came out of the wooded area and made his first attempt. She struggled with the killer, her sneaker came off. She escaped, ran, and he caught her where we found the body."

"Somebody must've heard her screaming."

"People have a tendency to ignore screams in the night."

"You're right, even if she did scream until her lungs busted nobody would have probably come to her aid anyway."

"Unfortunately that's the reality of the world we live in today."

Jones stood up and pulled his phone from his pocket; he called in the crime scene technicians.

Observing the openness, Jones walked towards the water fountain, he looked around.

"Brown look around, there's no entry point to this area of the park."

"Ok."

"I don't think she was followed… he was waiting for her here; the killer knew she would stop here."

"You think so."

"Had to be."

"So he knew her routine."

"Had to be… the boot prints are sunk in, indicating he stood in that spot for awhile. Knowing that at some point she would stop and take a sip of water."

"So what are you thinking, we have a strangler stalking women joggers in the parks of New York City?"

"Possibility, we'll have to pay them boys down at Compstat a visit and see if anything like this has crossed their path."

An hour later a white truck came bearing the insignia C.S.I. and made its way towards the detectives. The weight of the truck left deep tires tracks in the grass that stretched beyond the detective's sight.

Several men exited the vehicle. One of the men spoke and announced that he would be leading the crime scene team. A skinny white man dressed in a blue jacket that read police on the back, blue jeans that fitted tight around his thighs, tall, short hair cut, and his thin mustache made him look like an old western cowboy. Jones brought him up to speed. Now the entire south west and front entrances of the park were crawling with police.

"This is where it all started." Jones explained to the man, he pointed to the boot prints and sneaker prints. "Case those boot impressions. We'll need prints off the iPod also, and the sneaker." The crime scene personnel carefully cut the surrounding branches that partially covered the hideaway, and then they bagged the iPod and sneaker. Another set of C.S.I personnel dug deeply into the ground without disturbing where the boot prints were, carefully adding plaster in the deep impressions. In seconds the grayish liquid hardened and the men carefully lifted the impressions out of the ground with tools neither detectives saw before. A few hours later the crime scene investigators completed their task of photo taking, combing the area for any sort of evidence and casting the boot prints.

The area was now sealed off with crime scene tape, police cars stationed so that no one disturbed the crime scenes. Jones walked off the grass and focused his attention on the walking trail. There were light poles lined up all along the trail, benches, and a bathroom not too far away. The bathroom locked tight, the chain and lock rust covered. No video surveillance in the immediate area. No witnesses, no I.D. on the victim. The excitement of the investigation ran through Detective Jones body and unraveling the pieces of the puzzle fueled his desire to solve Jane Doe's murder.

Chapter 5

—

WEE HOURS...

Please visit facebook.com/AuthorJoeCarter or Amazon.
com to post comments. Have a question email me at
acarterpublication@gmail.com